The Consultant and the Cat

Jocelyn Aitkin

Chapter One

He supposed there were worse things in life than being followed by a big cat.

At the moment, Randolph couldn't think of any. He had thirty-two dollars to his name, and he'd just lost his second job in two months. He was angry with the cat, wanted to blame this one on the leopard. Of course, this wasn't entirely the cat's fault. Maybe he should never have saved the leopard in the first place, but no one deserved to be whipped and beaten close to death. So he saved the cat. Visiting her as she recovered hadn't helped matters, but after her first escape, he should have known that she wouldn't leave him alone. He'd had plenty of examples of the cat's ingenuity and determination. He should have known that she would follow him.

And, to give Kitty her fair due, she'd assisted in bringing a dangerous criminal to justice. His superiors just didn't see it that way. He'd tried to explain, but as he had promised that they wouldn't see Kitty again, they were rather unforgiving.

"You look beat," Marciano said, sliding into the seat across from him. "Bad day?"

"Oh, come on, Marcie," Randolph used the nickname that his best friend despised. He was angry. Simply put, Dalton Randolph had a temper, and it often got the better of him. The leopard growled, always attuned to his mood.

"Lay off, cat. He started it. Randolph, I know you're pissed because you got fired, but if you call me 'Marcie' again, I'll kill you," Marciano warned. Randolph knew it wasn't necessarily an idle threat. Marciano was two inches taller than Randolph's six-one and fifty pounds heavier. His family had connections to the mob—Marciano and his immediate family were all cops or feds, none crooked, but his cousins could make bodies disappear.

Randolph grunted, accepting Marciano at his word. They had been friends for years, close in age and roughly similar enough in appearance to be mistaken for brothers, other than the other man's gut, and yet Randolph still didn't know Marciano's first name. He watched, trying not to react to the anger that he felt when Marciano's coat opened, revealing his badge. Randolph used to have one of those. Now he didn't. "Look, you're not thinking straight. You're going about this all wrong. You didn't need to apply to the last *three* agencies. You're one of the best if not *the* best in your field. If you want them to, they'll come to you. That means you can set the terms, including one leopard."

Next to Randolph came the rumble of a growl-like purr. "Katya seems to like the idea."

Marciano smiled. "Good. I think I might have something for you. My cousin, Angelina, she's got a friend who's a cop. She's under a lot of pressure. High profile case. People think a woman can't handle it."

"And bringing me in on it will help?" Randolph demanded, shaking his head. The leopard put her head on his leg and looked up at him. He frowned.

"You're a consultant. It would be like asking the department shrink to compile a psych profile only better because you came up with it," Marciano insisted. "Let me call for you."

"Fine, call her if you like," Randolph said, getting to his feet. He left a tip on the table and started to walk away. He needed to sell his car, though he wasn't sure how people would react when he started walking around the streets with a leopard, and it might even be worse because she was a black one. Then there would be the taxi issue as well.

"Randolph, wait up," Marciano jogged up to him. Randolph suppressed a smile, trying not to laugh at the almost overweight FBI agent running down the sidewalk. Randolph's easy, unlabored stride had already put some distance between him and the restaurant. Marciano's new wife had been overzealous with the pasta, leaving him panting for a moment after he reached Randolph's side. "Don't tell me you'll do this and then back out. You need this, but it is *my* reputation on the line."

"I'll do it, damn it. Just don't ask me to like it."

"Dalton Randolph?"

"The third, actually," Randolph agreed with false cheerfulness, more of his Oxford accent slipping into his speech now that he was no longer angry or arguing with an Italian. He was aware that his name and accent gave him a rather pompous air, but he felt it best under the current circumstances. He declined to shake the mayor's overused hand and sat down. "This is Kitty."

The leopard padded over to the desk and climbed into the chair beside Randolph. The oil-slicked politician did his best to appear nonplussed, but he was scared. Years as a corporate lawyer had kept Thompson away from real danger, and those days were long eclipsed by his years in office. At the moment, Randolph would describe him as resembling a postman frightened by the sudden appearance of an unexpected dog.

"Kitty?" Thompson repeated, dumbstruck.

"I didn't name her. Trust me, it would have been a much better name if I had. I call her Katya as Levin did Kitty in *Anna Karenina,*" Randolph explained. The leopard gave him a bit of a purr.

"I don't remember that part."

4

Randolph sighed. "Honestly. No one seems to read that story line, but it's better than the Anna-Vronsky debacle. At any rate, Mayor, I've been asked to look into this serial rapist case, and I thought it best that you know that I have a leopard."

"A leopard?"

"Oh, don't let the black fool you. She *is* a leopard," Randolph said, trying to keep the conversation pleasant. "If you'd like my assistance, I need some sort of special dispensation for Katya, so please give me it."

"You have it," Thompson promised. "I want this matter resolved quickly. I'll have the paperwork you need by the end of the afternoon. Now, let's talk salary. How much is this going to cost? I made a pledge to the public that the best officer was on the case. I can't have an expensive, flashy out-of-towner taking the credit."

"Of course not," Randolph gave the other man a thin smile. "I don't want media exposure, just a good reference for my next job. I only require the salary that any other consultant would get, with part of it up front to tide me over. Perhaps a small additional fee to off-set the cost of my leopard. I'm not sure about that, but I believe we can work out terms that are very reasonable."

"You're kidding. Why did you go freelance if not for the money?" Thompson demanded, surprised. His plain greed came out in private, but he was one crooked politician among many, and Randolph didn't care whether or not Thompson's morals were what he claimed. "It's ridiculous. Freelance consultants are supposed to make the big money. It's the definition of freelance."

It wasn't, and that wasn't why Randolph was doing this. "I'd work for an agency if I could, but I can't. I have a big cat that follows me. It's hard to keep a job. I don't need to be rich, but the leopard *does* eat a lot. The real problem is the cat. Katya lost me my job with the ATF when she intervened in a bust, the DEA by blowing my cover, and the FBI by biting a suspect. No agency wants responsibility for me or Katya," Randolph explained. He saw the mayor's look and shook his head. "She is not a threat to your constituents. She will protect me to her death, that's all."

Katya licked his hand. Randolph smiled again. "All I want is employment. I can help with the case."

Thompson nodded. "Well, Doctor, I agree to your terms, on the condition that you have it put in writing that you are responsible for any actions taken by your leopard. I'm going to give you two weeks. I want daily updates. And you will not address the media. Ever."

"Understood. Now if I can have my paperwork, I need to meet Detective Reynolds in an hour."

"Stay in the car," Randolph warned, giving Katya his sternest look. The leopard stared back at him, blinking uncomprehendingly. He sighed. *"Please.* Please stay in the car. I'll only be a minute. I'll be fine. It's a police station. Perfectly safe. I promise."

He patted the dispensation in his pocket and headed into the police station. He'd wanted to appear as professional as possible as he could, since he had a leopard, so he'd worn his FBI "uniform" of black suit and dark tie. He'd brought his briefcase, the one that had been a present from Marciano when Randolph finished his PhD in psychology. Marcie had taken it upon himself to have someone stitch *'I don't suffer from insanity. I enjoy every minute of it'* on the lining. His friend's sense of humor was, in general, in bad taste. If anyone saw it, the image he'd hoped to cultivate would be ruined, but Katya would do that first, he was sure.

"Dr. Randolph?" a woman asked as soon as he was past the security at the door. She was waiting for him. Impatient, then. Went against her appearance, as did her voice. It had been more than a little deceptive. When he spoke to her on the phone, he had pictured a short, feisty brunette, not the tall, elegant woman before him. She made the plain business suit in pale cream look like an extension of her body, enhanced by the snow blonde hair, as if her clothing was more like her skin than just an outfit.

Meeting her cool blue eyes, he couldn't help asking, "Has anyone

7

ever told you you look almost exactly like the white witch of Narnia?"

She smiled in amusement. "Most men wait until they know me before they insult me. And once they know me, *no one* insults me."

"You are merely confirming my observation, Detective," he said, and she smiled frostily. "I've spoken to Mayor Thompson. If your superior asks, *he* asked for my help, not you. Assuming that you still want my help?"

"Angie says you're the best," Reynolds said with a shrug. "I suppose we'll have to see about that."

"I've actually never met Angelina. Er, wait. She was at Marcie's wedding. I guess I met her, but I don't know her. She doesn't know me," Randolph corrected. "I'll take a look at the files if you don't mind. And I need to see the crime scenes."

"The crime scenes we'll do after lunch," she told him, starting to walk away. "You can look over the files while you're here."

"That actually isn't a good idea. I was hoping to borrow them for a while."

"Not going to happen."

Randolph looked back at the door. No Kitty. Not yet. "You don't understand. I have a leopard."

"A *what?*"

"A leopard. *Pathera pardus.* She's melanistic, actually, so... black, but still a leopard. I worked with the FBI for several years. I was on a simple, seemingly straight-forward murder that turned out to be a part of a series of murders committed by a carnival worker—her trainer, to be specific. The bust went down at the circus; I had to stop him from whipping her to death. I saved her, that apparently bonded us, and now she won't leave me alone. She's become a sort of bodyguard. I tried to set her free. She couldn't adapt. I gave her to a wildlife preserve for animals that had been domesticated. She was home before I was," Randolph explained with a sigh. He shrugged. "She is my leopard, for better or worse."

"So... I have a profiler with a leopard?" Reynolds asked, trying to take this in stride. "Does the mayor know about this?"

"Yes. I have a special dispensation for her. And I accepted responsibility for her actions. Oh, and my words to the press are supposed to be 'no comment.'"

"I'm sure. Well—" Reynolds broke off as Katya joined them, pushing her head against Randolph's hand. "How did she get in here?"

"She's a very intelligent cat. Circus trained. She can roll down my car windows, and the outer door has a handicap access button," Randolph said. He looked down at the leopard and shook his head. "I told you I'd be fine, Katya. See?"

Reynolds looked at him. "Are you certain that you are a psychologist and not in *need* of one?"

"Would someone care to explain to me why there is a *panther* in my squadroom?" Lieutenant Bennett demanded as he stepped into the bull pen.

Persephone Reynolds looked up from her case notes, pushing a few strands of her hair behind her ear. She turned to the man occupying her desk chair. It was his leopard. He could explain. The accent would probably win anyone over—her mother would melt and tell Persephone to marry the man after only a few words. It didn't help that he had a strange, adorable leopard and was more or less good-looking. His eyes met hers, hazel and full of amusement, before he turned to the lieutenant and spoke.

"Actually, sir, she's a leopard," Randolph corrected. "It's a common misconception since she's melanistic—that is, black—but she is definitely a leopard and has spots. She's also the reason that I am here as a freelance consultant. She cost me my last three agency jobs. I finally figured that it was better to go into the private sector. I tell her to stay home, but she never listens. She was supposed to wait in the car, but you can see how well that worked."

He shrugged, feigning helplessness. Persephone thought his innocent act was decent. Bennett blinked, confusion and anger reddening his face. His overlarge gut, product of too many years behind a desk, heaved in a dangerous manner. He would start yelling in a minute, his perpetual indigestion fueling his ire. Randolph rose and extended his hand to the other man.

"Dalton Randolph the third. Forensic psychologist. I was called in to consult on this serial rape case. I *am* sorry about Katya. I thought if I was only gone long enough to pick up the case files, she wouldn't come looking for me," he explained. He looked over at the leopard and sighed. It purred. Well, it growled, but Persephone figured that was a purr since it didn't bother Randolph. "I was wrong."

Bennett looked at Reynolds. "You call him in?"

"No," she shook her head, giving him a half-truth. She hadn't called Randolph. His friend Marciano must have called Angelina, who called Persephone. She'd accepted the offer, though. She must have been desperate. "Must have been Mayor Thompson, sir."

"Election year," Randolph commiserated. The leopard came over and nuzzled his hand. Persephone found it somewhat endearing to see them interact. "See, Katya? I told you to wait in the car. You got me in trouble again."

"The mayor know about your... pet, Randolph?"

"Oh, yes, sir," Randolph handed Bennett a paper. Persephone assumed it was the special dispensation that he'd told her about earlier. Bennett read it over, scowling, cursed under his breath, and handed it back.

"Reynolds, take your consultant and his leopard and go find me a rapist," Bennett thundered, storming back into his office.

Randolph ran a hand through his dark hair and smiled at her. "I really am sorry about this. The cat, I mean. I'm supposed to be helping with the case, not causing more problems."

"Bennett is full of hot air. Most of it gas," she muttered, dismissing his apology. "You played him well, at least. We may as well visit those crime scenes now."

"Remember, to the press, it's no comment."

Randolph looked over at the white witch and sighed. "Did you honestly think I'd forgotten that? You assume I have anything to say to them, and I don't. I actually have nothing to tell anyone at this point. I barely got to read anything before your superior threw his fit and we had to leave. It seems very nearly impossible to get any work done with Katya around."

The leopard bumped his leg, and he looked down at her. "No, I'm not kidding, and no, I'm not amused. This is our best chance of making this work, and you're very close to ruining it."

Katya turned her big eyes on him and licked his hand. He forced himself to ignore the cat and focus on the woman. "Why are we discussing the press again anyway?"

"Now's the time when they're thinking about the afternoon editions and early news shows, so they tend to be camped out in front of the building, waiting for any of us to walk out and give them something they can use. I've had my picture on the news every night saying the same damn thing—that we're pursuing every angle and we hope to have more information soon," she explained, rubbing her forehead. Behind that cool demeanour of hers, the way this case was dragging on was getting to her. He wondered when the last time she'd slept was. "So now you've been warned. Say nothing."

He rolled his eyes. "Fine. I promise not to say a word. I can't make that promise for Katya. Do we honestly care if she bites anyone from the press?"

Reynolds looked at him for a moment, and he saw her fight a smile before she turned to go out and face the crowds. He patted the leopard on the head and followed the detective outside.

Her warning had been rather incomplete. He'd figured on one or two reporters, maybe two television crews, but all of the local news groups seemed to be out in full force, snapping pictures and asking questions. As soon as they saw him, they turned on him, demanding to know why he was there and where the leopard came from. He blinked and tried to push the microphones away.

"Kitty really doesn't like crowds, so if you could please back off," he began and got bumped. He heard a low growl from the leopard and winced. This was about to become very unpleasant. "Reynolds, love, perhaps since they are more familiar with you, you can persuade them to leave me alone before the leopard does something we all regret?"

They turned back on her, a new set of questions going her way. She raised her voice. "A connection to the case? No. The leopard is not a suspect. This is just... a man who works with a leopard. Kind of like a circus act, yes. Well, no, the cat is very adorable, isn't she?"

Randolph glared at the detective. She smiled as she came over to him. "I haven't forgotten you, though. The cat's adorable, but you..."

He frowned as she looped her arms around his neck, dragging his lips down to hers for a kiss. He supposed he looked like a complete fool, standing there as dumbstruck as he did, startled not only by her actions but by the fact that the ice queen wasn't *cold*. She didn't seem at all frosty, did not taste like a cool mint or something on that order as he would have expected. She was spice and fire and passion—only she'd done all this for show, so why the devil did it feel *that* good?

She let go and stepped back. "We should go, honey. I don't have long for lunch."

She took his hand and pulled him along through the crowd, and he had to wonder where the hell *no comment* had gone in that conversation.

Chapter Two

"It was a fit of pique," she repeated.

"A fit of pique? Good lord, woman, next time throw something like a normal human being," Randolph snapped, his irritation getting the better of him. "I am sure as hell not sticking to the 'no comment' rule after you tell the bloody press that I'm your boyfriend and work in the circus. I am—I have a doctorate in psychology. From Oxford. I do *not* work in a damn circus."

"Oh, you're just pissed because you got kissed by the white witch," she shot back, turning the car around the corner. He might figure she was driving too fast, but this was normal for her. She saw him grit his teeth and smiled.

His anger made him clip his words, changing his accent. "I don't care why you kissed me. Or *that* you kissed me."

He was protesting too much. Her implication—it wasn't really a statement—*had* rattled nerves. Randolph didn't like being her *boyfriend* more than he didn't like being said to work in a circus. And that kiss *had* thrown him off. He deserved it, between his pompous manner and the damn leopard. "I will have absolutely no credibility now. It's bad enough that Katya takes it from me, and she doesn't even mean to, but you—"

"I did what I had to do, Randolph. No one was supposed to know you were hired on for this case."

"You know I agreed to that. I don't need the limelight, but when they put this man on trial and ask me about my part in it, the press will already have put it out there that I am nothing more than... entertainment."

"You were almost a suspect. You *and* your leopard. Stop complaining and deal with it. It's not like you'll ever have to kiss me again. If anyone asks later, that was a deliberate mislead for the press and this sicko because we don't need him knowing that you—and your leopard—are on this case."

Randolph sighed, looking out the window. Persephone rolled her eyes. "You have a girlfriend?"

He snorted. "With Katya around?"

"So you don't have to worry about her getting upset and blowing it out of proportion. Me, on the other hand, my mother will be calling to demand I bring my new boyfriend home to dinner. Do not think I did this lightly. I just weighed the scenario, came up with a possible solution, and ran with it," Persephone told him. She sighed. She was not looking forward to her mother's inevitable response to the news, but the last thing she wanted was her case getting screwed up because of a damn leopard. She had yet to see anything from Randolph that proved he was worth this hassle, and if it didn't come soon, she was cutting him loose.

She stopped the car, parking it near the alley entrance. "We're here."

"This isn't where it happened," Randolph said, shaking his head as he opened the door. He got out and walked forward a few steps before looking back at her. "This is the dump site. Where he left her afterward because she was garbage to him. Used up and unworthy."

Persephone shuddered. It was unsettling voicing that thought aloud, but yeah, that was what this bastard had done. "We don't know where he takes them when he does it. He's abducted them from all over the place. Always leaves them in an alley."

"Near the trash. Disposing of them."

"Yes," Persephone agreed, watching the leopard walk up to him. Forensics had already been through here, so it wasn't like the cat could ruin anything. Katya put her nose to the ground and sniffed before circling around Randolph.

"I know, Katya," he said, touching the cat's head. It sat down next to him, and he sighed.

"She's really good at reading your moods."

He nodded, distracted, his fingers combing through the leopard's fur. "He's probably very close to escalating, Reynolds. He already sees them as trash after he's used them. It won't take much for him to move on to killing them when he's done."

"I know. Why the hell do you think I agreed to let you help me with this?"

"Headache?"

Randolph realized he was rubbing his forehead and stopped, looking over at Reynolds. He rose again, shaking his head. "I think I've gotten everything I can from these locations. I'll need to see the files."

"You look more like you've hit quitting time for the day."

"If your head doesn't hurt after walking in this guy's thoughts for a bit, there's something wrong with you. I don't care about compartmentalization. This stuff isn't something that should sit well with anyone. It should outrage us and shock us and keep us searching for the monsters that do it, not give them notoriety and fame for it," Randolph said, shaking his head as Katya bumped against him. "And I already know that the timeline's getting short. He's going to kill. Soon. Within... days. Maybe less than that. I go home now, and all I'm doing is setting myself up for a lifetime of guilt and regret for not doing everything I can while I still have a small chance of helping prevent it."

Reynolds nodded. "Now that you've seen all this, you have anything new?"

"He's... bold. The abductions are crimes of opportunity. He sees what he wants, waits for the moment he can get it—but not long, he doesn't have a long attention span. He's not a stalker. Most likely he saw her in that supermarket, headed out to his car, and waited. When she came out alone, having parked in a corner of the lot that was pretty much deserted, he saw his chance. He drove up, grabbed her, and that was it."

"He's smart enough to avoid the cameras, though."

"Impulsive but not reckless," Randolph agreed. Katya pushed at his leg, and he looked down at her. "Yes, I know you're hungry, love. We'll feed you and me, and I'll do some reading."

"I think that we still have the tapes from the store, even though they didn't have anything to tell us about her abduction."

Randolph looked at her. "Not on the surface, perhaps. It probably wasn't something where they even met. He saw her across the meat department or something, didn't pass close to her. He quietly paid, left, and waited. Maybe picked up a magazine on the way out so he'd seem less suspicious as he waited in the car."

Reynolds sighed. "Damn it."

Randolph nudged Katya and the leopard went over and licked her hand. Reynolds jerked a little, and he smiled. "Remember, the purpose of me being here is to point out what you might not have seen. You know most of this already."

"Let's get back to the station, then. I want to look at that tape, and you need those files. We can even contact our witnesses and arrange for you to speak to them."

"The victims? Not a good idea."

"You're a trained psychologist."

"And a man. With a leopard. It would be hard enough to talk to me in the first place, degree or no degree, but throw Katya in that mix, and I am bound to make things ten times worse for those women. I'll go through the files, find what I can and give you a list of questions to ask for me, but I'm not putting them through that."

"Surprisingly thoughtful of you."

He shrugged. "Not always, but this is a delicate situation, and the balance is going to tip quickly. I don't think these women are in any further danger from him because he doesn't see them as threats, as anything useful, but that's not going to comfort them. When he kills—and he's going to kill—they will start to fear for their lives and getting any further information or testimony from them will be difficult."

She nodded, taking out her keys. "You have something you want to pick up on the way back to the station?"

"I don't like to feed the leopard in public. Most people find the sight of her eating all that raw meat rather... unsettling."

"Fine. Your house. No, wait, you don't live here. Where are you planning on staying? It's not like a motel is going to accept your leopard."

Randolph winced. "Yes, well, I had... The plan was... unformed, to say the least."

"You were going to stay in your car?"

"Mostly. I would ensure proper hygiene, of course, but—"

"You are so going to regret this. *I'm* going to regret this. Get in the car."

"What?"

"Guess you get to meet my mother."

"Mom?" Persephone called as she opened the door to her parent's house, stepping inside. She still had a set of keys, as did her siblings, but she tended to be the only one around to use them. She leaned back to open the door for Randolph and the leopard. He wasn't kidding when he said that the leopard's eating habits were disturbing. She was a bit put off just by how much meat he'd picked up at the store. "She must be out. Go ahead and feed the leopard. I'll get the files and set them on the dining table."

"You're the only one with the light hair?"

Persephone shoved him into the kitchen with the food, thinking that was the best place for it since the tile would be easier to clean off after the meat. "No going through and analyzing my family. That's not why you're here."

He frowned, and Katya hissed a little as she passed Persephone. She willed herself not to react to the cat. She was not going to be intimidated by the leopard. "I merely found it curious. You have such distinctive features, but your siblings—"

"Look normal. And got normal names, too," she interrupted. "Yes, everyone thought I was adopted when I was growing up, but no, it's a bit of recessive genes coming into play. Comes with a wonderful skin condition. I go out in the sun uncovered, and I burn. More like a vampire than a witch, I guess."

Randolph surprised her by not making a comment after that one. He opened the package and dumped the meat on the floor for the leopard. Katya attacked it with a disturbing, vicious glee, and Persephone turned away from the kitchen, not wanting to look. She went to the car and grabbed the box from her back seat, carrying it inside to the heirloom table that her mother swore would be hers someday and started pulling out the files.

He joined her, wiping his hands on one of her mother's dish towels. "Katya will be busy for a while. This is usually when I take advantage of the distraction and shower."

"Must be quite the life with the cat."

"My own personal stalker," he agreed, tired. He looked at the files and shook his head. "I take it you're good with notes. Lots of details?"

"Well, each woman has three crime scenes plus the forensics from her personally and the statement she gave. It's quite a bit for each of them, and yet... Not enough."

"Did you lock the car? I think it's best if I get some food before I get too far into the files. I believe my blood sugar is a little low."

"You diabetic?"

"No, just hungry," he said with a slight smile. She shrugged as he left, taking each of the six files out and putting them in order from first to last. She wouldn't be surprised if there weren't a few missing, given the lack of reporting on crimes like this. She hoped those women would come forward and help end it—if only for their own peace of mind.

Randolph set the takeout containers on the table. "If you tell me where to find plates and silverware, I'll grab them so you can avoid the floor show."

"Cupboard next to the sink on the left and the drawer under it."

He nodded and went into the other room. She heard his voice and almost laughed. "No, Katya, I don't want to share. Thank you."

Persephone watched him come back with the dishes. "She's generous."

"It's disgusting, but yes."

Persephone smiled. He took out the containers and started dishing himself up a plateful. She blinked when he passed it over to her. "I can get my own."

"If you like," he said, shrugging. "I was attempting to be polite."

"Don't you get sick of people expecting that of you because of the accent? And the name?"

"The sad, sordid tale is actually that I am rather more American than English, and my only real claim to the name is that my father insisted on giving it to me if he was to fund my expenses at all. You see, he had a family already—no sons, mind you—and so in many ways I suppose my mother was fortunate to get anything at all from him. Generations of his family were educated in the best institutions in England, and that had to happen for his son as well, hence my accent, but I do believe I've only seen my father twice in my entire life."

"Nice."

Randolph shrugged. "The name has its weight and pretensions which can be used to my advantage, as can the accent."

"You sharing all that because I happened to call myself a vampire?"

He shook his head as he filled his own plate. "I live with a leopard and have given up on any illusion of having a private life. It is also a matter of public record. I do have a question, though. Why your

24

parent's home and not your own?"

"Not bringing a leopard into my apartment building. At least Mom has room here."

"Your father is dead?"

Persephone cursed. "I hate working with you shrinks. You're here to analyze the rapist, not me."

Randolph opened up a file and started reading, trying to keep his mind on the case and not the woman across from him. He had worked with a team for many years, and he had been comfortable with them. He had not been confronted with such open hostility for what he did in a long time, and he couldn't help wondering what made her so angry about it. He knew that many cops saw their department shrink as some kind of hindrance to their work, but he was not her enemy. He was here to help. He was on equal footing, held no power over her job except for the possible repercussions of Katya's presence.

He shook his head, closing the file. She looked at him. "No questions?"

"They didn't see anything."

She nodded. "They were drugged. None of them have any real memory of the actual rape, just a few flashes here and there. Nothing except they think he has dark hair because that's what the blur is—dark. I can't imagine that whole file tells you nothing, though."

Randolph reached for another file. "Oh, no, I'm picking up on his victimology, at the very least. He's rather specific, down to what they're wearing at the time he takes them. Another thing you already knew, though."

She lifted her plate, about to get up. He rose. "Let me. My leopard is still there, remember?"

She sighed, and he took his plate with hers into the sink. Katya was still working on her food, gnawing with contentment on the last of it. She'd made a big mess again. He let out a breath. "Katya, you have to stop playing with your food so much."

She blinked, and he shook his head as he walked back into the dining room.

"Do you always talk to her?"

He shrugged. "She's a constant companion, and it gives me some illusion of... control, I suppose. I have none, but I like to fool myself into thinking I do."

Reynolds leaned back in her chair, suppressing a yawn. He frowned again, reminded of his earlier observation that she probably hadn't been sleeping well—if at all. "You know, if you want to take a few hours, get some rest, you may feel free to do so. I do not need a babysitter—and if I did, I'm sure Katya would fill that role more than adequately."

Reynolds rolled her eyes. "Is everything about the leopard?"

"These days, yes."

Reynolds shrugged, closing her eyes for a moment. He went back to his chair and sat down again, opening up another file. He figured she'd stay there long enough to pass out, keeping watch over him, and if that was the way she had to do it, he would not try to stop her. He took the file and moved back to the entryway, to the picture of her family, frowning as he lifted the picture of the third victim to compare it to Reynolds' sister.

The white witch just might be lucky. The sister was this man's type. Granted, that photo was at least a few years old, probably ten, but the other girl was almost the exact same physical type.

"Persephone?" an older woman called, opening the door. He shut the file and prepared himself to face her mother. The older woman shifted her bag of groceries to her other hip and blinked at him with the same blue eyes. Other than them, she looked more like the other daughter in the photo, just further advanced in age. "Well, this is unexpected."

Randolph forced a smile. "My name is Dalton Randolph. I'm a consultant working with your daughter. I think she might actually have fallen asleep, though."

Mrs. Reynolds shook her head. "She hasn't slept in almost a week and—what the hell is that?"

"Katya," he said as he turned around, giving the leopard a pointed look. "There is nothing to worry about. Are you done eating? If you don't mind, Mrs. Reynolds, I would prefer to clean up after her before you see your kitchen."

"Uh..."

He took the bag from the woman. She was too stunned to object. "You have cleaning supplies, I assume? Something for your floor?"

"There's a leopard, and you want to clean my floor?"

"Yes."

To her credit, she didn't scream. She didn't faint. She just sat down right where she was. He looked at Katya and sighed. "You have to stop scaring people."

The leopard looked up at him and licked her lips.

Chapter Three

Randolph moved the shaken widow Reynolds into the living room, aware she was still in shock and Katya was not helping matters. He let her sit there while he found the cleaning supplies on his own— it would only be worse if she saw the red stains on her kitchen floor, and while he considered waking the younger Reynolds to help her mother, he opted against it because he did not believe she'd be willing to rest again if she was woken, even if that was probably the worst place she could have fallen asleep.

Katya's mess cleaned, Randolph returned to the lady of the house with a glass of water and held it out to her. "Does your daughter keep a room here?"

Mrs. Reynolds looked up at him. "My daughter? No. No, she needs her privacy from her meddling old mother, you know. She thinks I'll look at the pictures I shouldn't see and get upset and then don't even start on her personal life. I'm not allowed to discuss that with her."

Randolph nodded. "I see. Do you still have a spare room? She will regret that chair when she wakes up in the morning."

"Oh, you've got a couple hours at the most. She can't let go, that one. So responsible. So driven. Always needing to prove something."

"Spare room, Mrs. Reynolds. I'll move her in there if you have one. If not, I'd like to move her to the couch."

"Who are you again?"

"My name is Randolph. I'm a consultant. That is my leopard. The spare room—does it exist or not?" he asked, getting frustrated. He knew that the woman was still adjusting to the idea of the leopard in her house, but if she could just answer the question, it would make things much easier.

"Oh. Yes. I have two, actually. The girls used to share one, but now everyone's gone, and I've got a big house to myself. Except when my children come to visit. Then there's so many with all the grandchildren running around..."

Randolph forced a smile and walked away from her. She was still talking when he reached the dining room. The white witch was still asleep, thankfully, and he carefully picked her up into his arms, trying not to wake her as he did.

"Up the stairs, Katya. Find me the spare room."

The leopard did what he asked, bounding up in front of him, and he followed at a slower pace. He didn't figure that Reynolds would have been asleep if she'd gotten much rest before today—this deep sleep was probably borne of considerable exhaustion. She needed it far more than she'd admit.

Katya opened the second door with her nose, and he took Reynolds into it, setting her on the bed closest to the door. The leopard sniffed around some more, hopping up onto the other bed and curling up. He gave her a look. "Nap time?"

She closed her eyes, and he shrugged. He had better deal with the mother and get back to the files.

He started down the stairs again, finding the other woman waiting for him. "No one else she works with would dare do that."

"I'm not staying. This is only for a specific case," he explained. "They're terrified because they actually have to work with her beyond the one. I don't."

Mrs. Reynolds nodded. "Yes. I see. I'm Lillian. Does the leopard have a name?"

"Katya. They named her 'Kitty' of all things, and I had to change it."

"Is she housebroken?"

He took a deep breath. "Well, that really depends on your definition. Oh, she is aware of the need to go outside, and she has learned not to chew the couch, but we're still working on her etiquette with guests."

"Oh?"

"She's a very possessive leopard."

"So... Are you single?"

Randolph didn't look up from the notes he was making. "I had a girlfriend. Now I have a leopard. Is there something I can help you with, Lillian?"

"Just curious. My daughter doesn't often bring people home, and even when she does, most of them do not have a leopard."

He reached for his water and took a sip. He was sick of the leopard consuming every facet of his existence. He was not a person anymore; he was a leopard keeper. It was entirely different. Exhausting. Infuriating. It was not that he disliked Katya, but there were still times when he wished he hadn't saved her simply because of the mess she'd made of his life and how he barely felt like he'd had the space to breathe since she came into it.

"Mom, leave him alone," Reynolds said, coming into the dining room again. She was a mess and had not gotten enough rest as she should have. She stopped and looked at the clock above the table. "You're kidding."

He followed her gaze and shook his head. "That has to be broken. I do not believe you've been asleep nearly long enough, and I have... I suppose this is the last file, and I have several pages now of notes, but it's not that late."

"Wishful thinking on both your parts," Lillian said as she got to her feet. "I'll have you know I set a new record and did not ask this one any questions for two full hours and then it was just if he was thirsty."

"That true?"

Randolph nodded. "I suppose it must be, but if you need to, you may be comforted by the knowledge that she was in shock over the leopard for a good part of that time."

The white witch smiled at him and went over to her box. "Where are my tapes? I need to go through that footage again. I don't expect a lot given the equipment they had, but after you pointed out that he was there—"

"Probably there. What I do isn't an exact science. People don't always fit the profile or the profile fits the wrong person as well as the right one," he reminded her, rubbing the back of his neck. "A profile is just a place to start looking and is *not* admissible as evidence."

"Sways the jury often enough."

"It is not conclusive proof, though. Things will match up, but they're still vague enough to let that happen," he said, reaching over to pet Katya as she came up to him. She pushed the chair next to him out and jumped onto it, startling Lillian. The white witch just shook her head. "Yes, yes, I was talking about your monster, Katya, but you know he can't hurt you now."

She started purring, licking him on the cheek. He grimaced. "I thought we discussed that. Not the face. We agreed."

She ignored him, as always, and he sighed, rubbing his head. He reached for the list he'd compiled and passed it to Reynolds. "I'd like you to ask them about those things, try and see if anything jogs in any of their memories."

She read it over with a frown. "You want to know what laundry detergent they used?"

Randolph hesitated, giving the mother a look. Reynolds echoed it, and the older woman sighed. "Fine, fine, I'm going."

After he heard her on the stairs, he looked back at the detective. "Sensory trigger. Each of the women said they were wearing a sundress when he took them. In every case, though, he dumped them without it. Something about the dress is key to why he picked them."

"And you think it was the way they smelled?"

"It's possible. It could be the cut since not all of them mention any kind of patterning to the dress and most mentioned different colors, but if it was just the style..."

"Then what?"

He put his pen down and reached for the water again. "Then I think he'd have a lot more victims given the change in season. More and more women are opting for summer clothing as the temperature rises. Sundresses seem to be everywhere, and he targets blond women in their early twenties. In a college town like this, he has plenty to choose from, even with many students off and back home for the summer."

"So you think it's more?"

Randolph let out a breath. "The women themselves are roughly the same size, around the same age, and have the same color hair, but their face shape and eye colors are different. I doubt he sees the faces. It's a bit early for me to make an assumption like this..."

"What?"

"I think he's recreating a moment of rejection. A specific blond in a specific sundress rejected him, and he's using these women as substitutes. In the end, though, he knows they're not the one he wants, so he dumps them like garbage after he's done using them."

Reynolds winced, sitting down. "So are we looking for the woman or for the man?"

"The woman could lead us to him... Or there's a reason he hasn't gone after her already."

"Like... she's dead?"

"Possibly."

"You have anything on him yet?"

"Few things, nothing cohesive yet. I'm not holding anything back, Reynolds. When I have something, you'll know it. It's just that not everything adds up right away. It's easier to see why he might have gone for these women because I have information on them. I've got almost nothing on him. Just a few inferences that aren't enough to pin down a personality."

"I think it's your turn to sleep. I'm going to look through those videos while you let those ideas work into something cohesive."

Persephone stopped in the doorway, and the leopard looked over at her. She met the cat's eyes head on, still unwilling to be intimidated. "You always stand guard like this when he sleeps?"

The leopard opened her mouth, showing her teeth. Persephone looked back at Randolph, turning in agitation on the narrow bed that was too short for him, wondering if it was this case that had him worked up or something older. Though the question of *why* always haunted her, she had never wanted to do what he did, look right into the minds of these creeps. She knew that it was important, but she would much rather follow the trail of evidence instead. Evidence tended to be cut and dry without any gray area. This case was frustrating because it left them very little to work with.

Even Randolph's new lead with the supermarket video hadn't panned out. She hadn't seen anything that helped. The only other option would be checking on everyone who'd shopped in the store that day, but the guy could have paid cash and not been a part of a store loyalty program. He wouldn't be. He was careful. Never left anything behind, never gave them anything they could use.

"I'll leave you to it," Persephone told the cat, and the leopard blinked at her. She got the unpleasant feeling that the cat understood *plenty*. Persephone shook her head as she went back downstairs. She crossed back to the kitchen and went for a cup, taking it out of the cupboard on the right of the sink and setting it on the counter.

"Coffee's fresh."

"Mom, what are you doing up?"

"You brought a leopard into my home and honestly expect me to sleep?" Lillian asked, incredulous. She shook her head. "That's out of the question. I'm surprised you did."

"I don't think that leopard is a danger to anyone unless they threaten Randolph—which no one here would do," Persephone told her, filling her cup and going into the dining room to sit down. Her mother followed her with her own cup, sitting down across from her.

"I hope you're right about that," Lillian said. She looked at the box on the table and shook her head. "There are times when I really wish you'd never decided to become a cop."

"I figured that was your intention, what with you naming me Persephone and all," she observed with a slight smile. Her mother rolled her eyes.

"It had nothing to do with your chosen profession. And if you put the myth into it—"

"I'm still single, Mother, and I'm not married to death, even if I am a cop." Persephone shook her head as her phone rang and her mother gave her a pointed look. She sighed as she took it out of her pocket. "Reynolds."

She listened and then let out a curse, ending the call. She got up, leaving the dining room, and taking the stairs two at a time until she reached the leopard. "Go wake him?"

Katya blinked. Persephone gave the cat a dirty look. "Well, you're in my way. Either wake him or move so I can. Randolph!"

The leopard went over and jumped on him. He groaned. "Katya... Can't breathe when you do that. Get off."

Persephone found herself wanting to smile despite everything. "We need to go."

"Now?" Randolph asked, trying to get up around the leopard. "Another victim?"

Persephone nodded. He cursed.

Chapter Four

"I hate when I'm right."

"You do?"

"About something like this? Always," Randolph said, shaking his head. Persephone pulled on her gloves and nodded, looking toward the alley again. She didn't like this. It wasn't that she thought this thing had anything to do with Randolph—though to be safe, she had verified his story after the leopard showed up, and he *was* working in another state when this thing started—but she still didn't like that this had happened almost after he got here.

"You coming?"

"Katya will follow me. I'll wait until forensics has finished what they're doing. Besides, the press should probably see me on this side of the tape," he answered, putting his hands in his coat pocket.

Persephone moved away from him, ducking under the tape and moving past the uniformed officer stationed at the edge of it. He would keep the press back, though the damage was really already done. They had already connected this to the man she was hunting, and the story would be everywhere soon enough.

She reached the dumpster and the other detective. "What do we have, BB?"

Batscher pointed to the sheet. "Our first body. And she's a mess. Homeless man found her. We already rounded him up and took him to the station."

"Feed him, make sure he's sober, and then I want to talk to him," she said, kneeling down next to the sheet. She lifted it up and winced as she set it back down. "Why haven't they moved her? Waiting for me?"

BB shook his head. He was in a better state than Randolph, and she had to wonder what he'd been doing all day while she took the profiler through this mess. "Your new partner."

"Jealous?" she asked, and Bryson shot her a dirty look. She shrugged. They both knew he didn't enjoy working with her, and this case was the only reason he was willing to put up with her. It was too big for one person to handle alone, and she knew that they weren't far from appointing a taskforce. As it was, they'd been borrowing people from all over the place to track bits and pieces of this down. She had lead—not because they trusted her with it but because the media had latched onto her—and because the victims were more comfortable with her than any of her male colleagues.

"When'd you call in the feds, anyway?"

"Randolph isn't a fed anymore. He's independent, and he's got a pretty good handle on this so far."

Batscher scoffed, wrinkling the skin around the bump in his nose from being broken one too many times. "Took out the magic shrink ball and found out how to melt the ice queen?"

"This is a crime scene, Batscher. Don't make me hit you," Persephone warned, her voice tight. "That was for the press. I don't want it public that we brought in a profiler. Not yet. I want this guy thinking he's a step ahead of us. Getting overconfident. I want him screwing up."

"Yeah."

Persephone shook her head, looking at the sheet again. "Canvas turn up anything?"

"Usual amount of nothing. We're pulling the footage from all the traffic cameras again, but he left us the same as he always does. Zilch. When's the shrink going to stun and amaze us, then?"

Persephone stood, leaning around BB and calling across the crowd. "Randolph, You think you can ditch the cat for a minute?"

BB frowned, and Randolph turned to the cat before crossing the tape. "Randolph, this is Bryson Batscher, one of the other detectives on this case. BB, Randolph. You were right. About the what you said at the first dump site. And a few other things."

"She doesn't have a face, does she?" Randolph asked, moving over to the sheet, and Persephone nodded to his back as Batscher continued to frown. "He leave the dress this time?"

"No," Batscher answered. "Part of the reason we figure this was him, other than the dump site. You can look at the body yourself and see."

Randolph gave the detective a look. "Yes, but you're testing me at the moment, so I'll forgo that for what else I can observe before you— Very funny, Katya."

They all looked up then, and BB jumped back when he saw the leopard on the fire escape. She bared her fangs at him, and Randolph shook his head. "Be nice. I told you to stay put."

"Cat... Big... Cat," Batscher managed to say, and Persephone rolled her eyes. She looked at Randolph. He shrugged.

"At least she didn't get close to the body, right?"

"Close enough."

"He killed her with something impersonal, something that put him at a distance. He didn't need to feel the kill, just wanted her gone."

"Shot her in the chest," Persephone agreed. "You going to look under that sheet now?"

Randolph gave the leopard another glance and lifted the sheet, taking in the body with a wince. "Bashed her face in but killed her at a distance... He lost his temper for the first bit, but he calmed down afterward. He pulled back, distanced himself—Cold. He wants to be cold. Wants it to have no effect on him. Right now, he believes it does."

"Meaning he's not going to slip up anytime soon."

"He did. What he did to her face is proof of that," Randolph disagreed, putting the sheet back down. "That was done with his bare hands. Maybe a forensic anthropologist can reconstruct the damage he did and get more of a sense of him physically. Who found her?"

"Homeless man. I'm going to talk to him when the coroner takes the body. BB, what did Ollie have to say about the body? How long has she been dead? How long between when she was dumped and when she was found? She clearly wasn't killed here."

"Uh..."

"Guess you'd better talk to the coroner yourself. I'm going to the end of the alley, Katya, you... Damn it."

"What?"

"Look at her."

"Yeah, the leopard's pissed. I figured that was either BB or your mood."

"No, he was here. She's not the only one using the rooftops. He probably watched over all of them, waiting for them to wake or someone to find them."

She frowned. "Thought you said they were trash to him, that he didn't care what happened to them after he used them."

"It's what he wanted it to look like, at least. I told you—This isn't an exact science..."

Randolph trailed off, looking around in agitation. Persephone heard the leopard growling. That was no purr. The cat was angry. She read the profiler's moods, and he was definitely off. Persephone touched his arm. "Randolph?"

He shuddered. "I really hate when they watch."

"He's still here?"

Batscher pulled himself out of leopard shock long enough to start issuing orders, trying to close down the perimeter and get someone up to the rooftop. Randolph shook his head. That was going to take way too long. By the time anyone got up there, the man watching them would be long gone. He looked at Katya.

"Go."

She started climbing up the stairs, and he tried to relax. Reynolds looked at him. "You okay?"

"It's... a very thin line before you get too close to any of this stuff. When they watch, it's worse. Makes that line feel... non-existent," Randolph admitted. He was not going to go into the details. Those things were best forgotten. He looked toward the press again. "So much for them not publicizing my involvement, right?"

"I can't think of a way to salvage the situation at the moment,"

44

Reynolds agreed. "You think Katya will find him?"

"Not sure. We'll know soon enough. If she lost him, she'll turn back and come find me. Her first priority is always protecting me."

"I noticed. She stands guard when you sleep."

"Creepy, isn't it?" Randolph asked, moving out of the way as the coroner and his assistant came for the body. He walked toward the back of the alley and shook his head as he studied his surroundings. "There's only one way in. One way out. Why would he do that, block himself in like that?"

"He's up on the roof, remember?"

"But the only reason that Katya didn't jump down to where I was when she got on that fire escape is that it doesn't go down far enough—a reason to speak to the building manager and get that violation fixed—so it's not like he climbed up there to get away. If someone had seen him on the way out... It doesn't make sense. One minute he's careful, the next he's not."

"You look like you're going to break your own brain trying to figure this one out."

Randolph frowned. "That why you stayed here instead of going off to search for him?"

"He was gone before BB started talking. The minute you knew he was up there—as soon as Katya did—he had to have taken off," Reynolds said, defensive. "I wouldn't have been any faster getting up there than people who were already on the move. And yeah, you looked more than a little rattled after you said he was watching. What happened the last time?"

"Saw too much. Figured out things no one wants to know. Solved the case but had a nervous breakdown. Typical of my line of work, really," Randolph answered, moving back toward the press. He had no intention of talking to them, but the alley had nothing more to tell him right now. Forensics would give them more—he hoped.

Reynolds followed him. "You sure you can handle this? Because if you can't—"

"I'm fine."

She gave him a doubtful look. He knew she had no reason to trust him on that, but that case was years in the past, and it was only the feeling that he was being watched that unsettled him. It wouldn't happen again. "I don't think you are."

"You want to talk about how your father dying led to you becoming a cop?"

"Hell, no," she snapped, and even as she said it, he could see the question go through her mind, asking herself how he'd known that, wondering if her mother had said anything. He didn't have details, but this was what he did. He was very good at interpreting what he saw and heard. He could fill in the blanks.

"Was it a robbery? Maybe in a convenience store?"

"Damn you, Randolph. I told you not to analyze me."

She stalked away, pretending she was going to talk to the coroner before he left with the body. Randolph shrugged. She'd pushed him, so he pushed right back.

Katya came up to him, dropping a piece of fabric on the ground in front of him and starting to purr. He reached down to pet her. "Good girl. Very good girl."

"Honeymoon over?"

"Screw you, BB. I am not doing this. I told you what that was, and you can stop giving me crap about being a 'traitor' and calling in a consultant, even if he's a damn pushy shrink," Persephone snapped as they walked toward the morgue.

"Ooh, you pissed her off," the other detective said, turning back to look at Randolph. He shook his head. "Better watch out. She might just hurt you before this case is over."

Randolph gave the other man a look. "You assume quite a lot there, Batscher. Not only do I walk around with leopard, as soon as I give you a profile, I'm done."

Persephone stopped and looked at him. That wasn't the attitude he'd had earlier. "So, what, now you run off as soon as it hits a bit close to home? He watched you so you back off and leave as soon as you can? What happened on that case that makes you so damn scared?"

Randolph glared at her. "You want me to ask about your father again or shall we call a truce, one where you stop asking me about that case and I stop asking you about him?"

"You are so dead," BB muttered, backing away from the profiler. The leopard moved toward him, and he jumped back toward Persephone. She rolled her eyes.

"My father has nothing to do with this case. Your issues apparently do."

"To which I would counter by inquiring exactly how many murders either of you have worked. When you have come close to my current tally, then I think we may reassess this conversation, but I assure you, if I felt that I was incapable of working this case, I would simply have refused to do so as I have done in the past."

"The leopard thing doesn't make you a little bit... I don't know, desperate?"

He laughed. "Not in the way you think, trust me. Come, Katya. We are not wanted here. We can find other ways of keeping busy, yes? If only you could describe the man you chased. That would be most helpful. Not that I think he'd be in there—this rapist is probably not a man who has crossed anyone's radar before—but shall we go look at

48

pictures anyway? You can laugh at the mug shots."

The cat looked up at him, licked his hand, and started to purr. He smiled at her and walked off in the opposite direction.

BB shook his head. "We have a lunatic for our profiler. We can't use anything he gives us."

Persephone sighed. "He's a bit... off, but he said this guy was going to kill only hours before he did. He figured out how the third victim was taken from the supermarket. And he spotted the fact that we were being watched in that alley. None of the rest of us did. Not to mention that his leopard managed to get us our first real piece of forensic evidence. We don't have to like him, BB, but he seems to be pretty good at what he does."

"Even with the crap he's giving you about your dad?"

"I made one comment about my mother having room, and he knew my father was dead. He jumped from that to my dad's death being the reason I became a cop, asked if he died in a robbery, and my mother swears that she didn't tell him a damn thing. It pisses me off, but the man does... *know* things. More than I want him to know. If he can pick up on that kind of crap... Then I think he'll help us bring this bastard in. I can handle Randolph as long as he sticks to the damn case."

"Maybe."

Persephone ignored him as she went into the morgue. Doctor

Oleneva waved them over. "Thought you'd have a few other guests for me."

"The lovebirds are fighting," BB told him. Persephone looked around for the nearest bit of blood to point out to him. BB was many things, and squeamish was one of them.

"Shut up, BB. Ollie, what have we got?"

"Death was the result of one gun shot to the chest, almost merciful considering what he did to her face. If she'd survived, she was probably looking at brain damage and a long series of surgeries to rebuild her face. He completely destroyed her bone structure, and she could have died from the trauma to her skull, but he stopped her heart first."

Persephone shook her head. "This guy isn't merciful, Ollie. He's twisted. That is—if we're sure he's the same guy."

"Still waiting to get back the labs, but I suspect we'll find the same drugs in her system, and she was definitely assaulted. There's tearing, but no DNA. Typical of this guy's work as I understand it."

Persephone cursed. "Anything else?"

"We have the bullet, and ballistics will be able to tell you more about it."

She frowned. Something was nagging at her, and as much as she didn't like it, she thought she might have to ask Randolph about it. "Any chance of identifying her?"

"No match to any missing persons report yet."

"There wouldn't be. He doesn't hold them for that long, damn it. He probably grabbed her early this morning, maybe in the afternoon, and now she's gone."

"Got anything?"

Randolph looked back at Reynolds and forced a smile, passing her a sheet he'd printed out. "Katya growled at this one. Whether that means anything or not is entirely debatable. I sometimes catch her doing that at the television."

"That leopard might be the best witness we have. Go check this guy out, BB."

"Are you kidding me? I have to go look into a bogus lead brought up by a *leopard?*"

Katya opened her mouth, moving toward the other detective like she might just attack him. Randolph stood. "Leave him alone. He doesn't know how smart you are, but Reynolds is giving him a chance to see first hand."

Katya stopped. She looked at Batscher again and then turned and licked Reynolds' hand before coming back to stand next to Randolph's legs. Batscher gave the cat another look, shaking his head. Reynolds folded her arms over her chest. "Would you rather deal with our homeless man? Because it's either the leopard's lead or Mr. Stinky. Your choice."

Batscher went back to his desk, grabbing a coat. Randolph looked at her with a slight frown. "Is someone—exactly what gives you the right to such blatant prejudice, anyway? You have no reason to make judgments about why this man has no home."

"His problem is the smell. BB has no stomach for anything," Reynolds intervened, though they both knew it went deeper than the man's sense of smell. "Are you coming this time?"

"Katya and I will watch from the observation room, and if I think of anything, I should be able to join you without her following me. Or so I would hope," he said, running his fingers through the leopard's fur. She gave Batscher another flash of her teeth as she passed by him, eager to follow Reynolds toward their interrogation room.

"The coroner wasn't able to tell us much," Reynolds informed him as they walked along. "The facial damage was extensive, could have been fatal on its own."

"So you want to know why he would have shot her?"

"Is it the need for detachment you mentioned earlier?"

"The rage he felt when he turned against her and beat her face was... primal. He wants to be more rational. Still, he has to know what he's doing isn't rational. He can't replace the woman he wants no matter how hard he tries."

Reynolds stopped just outside the room. "You think she's dead?"

"It would seem more likely, since he's started killing her proxies, but that doesn't guarantee it. He could be working up to confronting her."

"Gaining confidence with each woman he takes and now with each one he kills?"

Randolph nodded. "There could be a lot more bodies coming."

Reynolds shook her head. "I want him before that happens."

"If this woman is alive, she could narrow it down for us, but chances are, she doesn't even remember the incident. It happened so fast for her, an ordinary occurrence. She was flirted with, turned the man down for whatever reason she might have had, and left. She probably has no idea the effect she had on him."

Reynolds took a deep breath. "Even asking for a specific date and incident—if we had it, and we don't—probably wouldn't get us anywhere, then."

"It's unlikely," Randolph agreed. "And if, as the victimology suggests, this incident happened in college, the woman he fixated on could be across the country by now, having long since graduated and moved on—if she isn't dead."

Reynolds turned to the door again. "You think your leopard is right about that mug shot?"

Randolph glanced back at Katya and sighed. "If she is, it's not our rapist. Maybe some kind of... wannabe or fan, but that young man had a bunch of petty crimes we wouldn't see from the man we're looking for. This one... He's the type that when it comes out will shock everyone. No one will want to accept that they never saw the monster underneath the surface."

"One of those charmers, someone everyone loves?"

"Quiet type, never causes a stir. This guy was never popular, but those that know him like him. That was what made her rejection that much harder to take. She seemed to like him, but she said no," Randolph added. He caught something in Reynolds' face and frowned. "What is it?"

She shrugged. "Guess I'm lucky. Never could wear any kind of sundress."

Randolph considered bringing up the possibility of her sister, but before he had made up his mind, she had gone into the interrogation room. He went over to join Katya where they could both watch. "You're drooling. What is it now?"

The leopard put her paws on the glass, studying the room with intensity, and he wondered if she was able to smell whatever might be on the man in the other room. "I suppose we need to feed you again."

"So clean."

Persephone tried to control her temper as she looked at the man across the table from her. They'd told her he was sober, but he couldn't be. She didn't know why they thought this crap was funny, but she would make them pay for it later. This was unacceptable. "Mr. Jenks, I need you to focus. You have to tell me about the woman you found in the alley."

"So clean."

Persephone shook her head. "You mean the body? It was clean?"

"You, Reynolds. Even if the suit's wrinkled, he's afraid to talk to you because he'll get all that white dirty," Randolph said as he walked into the room. She looked up at him, not liking the fact that he'd pointed out to her. She had forgotten what she was wearing—she didn't even have time to think about it on the rare occasions when she made it home these days. She wanted tell the guy just how clean the suit wasn't, but she doubted that would help.

"Mr. Jenks, is it?" Randolph asked, sitting on the corner of the table. "Can we ask you about the woman whose body you found?"

Jenks looked at Randolph like he just might answer, but then he frowned and looked back at Persephone. She sighed. "Randolph, give me your coat."

He stood, taking it off and passing it to her. She put it on over her suit, and Jenks stopped staring at her. He looked down at his hands and held them out to her. "I was afraid to touch her. So dirty. Can't touch anything."

Persephone nodded, hoping they could get this interview over as fast as possible. She was going to roast with Randolph's coat on over her damn suit. She hated warm weather. She had to dress so that she covered most of her skin and didn't get sunburned, and most days she felt like she spent the entire time close to passing out from the heat when she was out at a crime scene. Being indoors—at the police department, at least—was almost worse because the air conditioning never seemed to work.

"Mr. Jenks, how did you find the woman? Is that alley... always your home?" she asked, trying to get control of the interview again. "Are you there... all the time?"

"Can't go anywhere else. Not clean."

"Did you see what happened when the woman came? Was there a man who brought her there?"

The old man lowered his head and started crying. Persephone shook her head. She no longer thought the man was drunk. Now she understood. He seemed to be suffering from some kind of illness or trauma. She looked at Randolph. This was his field, wasn't it?

"Everyone needs to eat," Randolph began in a gentle tone, looking at the man with sympathy. He walked over and knelt beside him. "You went to get food and when you came back she was there?"

The old man nodded. "Collected a lot of cans. Had enough for a real meal for a change. Treated myself to it."

"And there is nothing wrong with that," Persephone told him. "This is not your fault. She was dead before he brought her there. You couldn't have saved her."

The old man shook his head. "Was my home. He never should have put her there. But I don't know who he is. Didn't see him."

"We'll find him," Randolph said, getting to his feet again. He shook his head as the door opened. "Katya. You shouldn't be here."

Jenks looked over at the leopard. "Here, kitty. Pretty kitty."

The leopard walked over and put her head in the man's lap, and he held onto her, petting her as he continued to cry. Randolph walked over to Persephone and nudged her toward the door. She walked out with him, shutting the door behind him and giving him back his coat. She pulled off her suit jacket and fanned herself a little.

"You consider registering that cat as a therapy animal?"

"Doesn't work with everyone."

"I think it's time to start in on damage control."

Reynolds looked at him. Her face and posture betrayed how

exhausted she was, but Randolph knew that he would never convince her to rest again this soon after the discovery of the first body. These hours were critical, but they were the hardest, even more so for someone already feeling the physical strain. "The six living victims need to see you, need to know that you haven't stopped looking for this guy and that you will do everything you can to protect them. In the light of the discovery, yesterday's fit of pique is going to set you back with all of them. Not only that, but I need to feed Katya again, and both of us could use some food. I suggest a brief regrouping— everyone will eat, you will shower and change so that you present the right image, and then you will have to speak to them. You do have patrol cars watching their houses?"

Reynolds nodded, rubbing the back of her neck. "Yes. I'll try and arrange for them to get doubled, but none of that will matter if we can't find this guy."

Randolph leaned against the wall for a moment. "Is there anything you can think of that you haven't already done?"

"No, but that's the hard part. I can't help thinking that I have to be missing something. Something stupid that I'll kick myself for later."

"You've been a cop long enough to know that always happens."

She sighed. "This is my first case like this. We don't *get* cases like this around here. A bit of gang violence, a few stupid kids, domestic calls, but a guy like this? A serial offender? This is new. It's scaring everyone. It's not something we know how to deal with, not that anyone wants to admit that."

"These cases are not isolated to big cities."

"Thanks. That makes me feel so much better."

He shook his head. "I'm not—the reason I'm saying this is not to scare you. I just meant that even a large city or a field office would *not* have any more experience than you have here. Serial killers are not as common as the books and movies and television shows would lead you to believe. It's just that one murder stopped being scary a long time ago. They need more kills to increase the hype because we've become convinced that a single murder can be solved in less than an hour thanks to those television shows. You've heard of the CSI effect, haven't you?"

"Yes. Juries letting criminals off because the case doesn't have all the DNA and forensics and a confession that that those shows somehow manage to find in every single case. Not that I watch it. I don't. I find that crime shows piss me off."

"Same here. People in my profession are shown as either manipulative department shrinks that keep the good cops from doing their jobs or as something closer to a damn psychic, jumping to a conclusion without even the right *inferences* to make it."

"You jump to plenty of conclusions."

Randolph supposed it seemed that way. "I don't always explain it, but I have my reasons for what I say. I have training and statistics to back them, usually. On occasion, there's a blind hunch, a conviction that doesn't fit with the rest of it. I don't ignore them, but I tend to hold them back until I have more than my... gut to suggest it."

"You have one of those here?"

"Maybe."

"But you won't share it?"

"Right now, it's a waste of time that we do not have. Instead, I think it best we focus on what we can actually do, and that includes talking to the previous victims again. It's not just for their sake you need to talk to them. With the drugs, it's unlikely that they'll remember anything new, but even the smallest, most random thing can be the connection that makes the rest of it fit."

"Speaking of the drugs, while we're still here, I need to check in with the narcotics team and see if they got anywhere tracking down what he's using. That'll give Jenks a few more minutes with your leopard before we let him go."

"I'll wait here."

Persephone ran a brush through her hair again and twisted it back into a bun, letting out a sigh. Randolph had some expectation of her reassuring those women, but she didn't think she'd have any chance of doing that right now. She looked even more washed out than usual, like the white witch he'd called her when they first met—though he was far from the first person to make the connection. Hell, her parents had named her after an ancient Greek myth because of her hair and complexion. She looked different, so she got the unique name, as if it wasn't hard enough looking like a bleached out version of her older sister without the weird name.

This suit didn't help any. Too much contrast. She looked even paler when she wore a strong color, but she hadn't managed to find time even to take clothes to the dry cleaner's. She could have asked her mother, she supposed, but she hated drawing her family into this kind of thing.

She walked downstairs to the familiar smell of her mother's cooking, shaking her head. Lillian shouldn't even be here, and she did *not* need to be cooking for them. "Mom, what are you doing?"

"Cooking breakfast in my own home. Not a crime, Persephone."

"Where's the leopard?"

"On the back porch. Honestly. It was a simple solution."

"For you, maybe, not your neighbors," Persephone told her, shaking her head. She grabbed a cup of coffee and went in to join Randolph. "You did inform her that your pet's eating habits are going to scare the neighborhood, right?"

"I did. She insisted on having her kitchen. You look terrible."

"Thanks a lot."

He sighed. "I did not mean it as an insult. However—"

"I look about as reassuring as death warmed over. I know," she muttered, shaking her head. "Mom, will you do me a favor and take some of my suits over to the dry cleaner's? I just... keep forgetting, and I'm almost completely out of things to wear."

Randolph looked at her. "Can you forgo the suit jacket and take down the hair? I think that will help. The hair, at the very least. Far too severe."

"It'll be in my way the entire time."

"Put it up after you talk to them. This really is no time to look like the white queen," he said, rising. He came around the table and undid the barrettes she'd used to pull back the strands at front that always came loose and took them down to frame her face. "Better. Not nearly as harsh. I still say lose the jacket if you can."

"I am not—"

"Act like the ice queen in front of the press if you like. Use it against the idiots in your department, but not those women. This is not about professionalism. It is about them."

She glared at him. "I don't care if this is about national security. Do not touch me again."

"You crossed that boundary first, remember? This is tame

compared to what you did. If we were going to discuss which of us has a stronger case for sexual harassment, I'd win, but that is not my concern at present. I would rather you didn't look half as exhausted as you do now, but there's no way you'll agree to sleep, so we will simply work with what we've got. You're going to overcome the fact that this already terrifying man from their worst nightmare has begun killing—"

"And you. And your leopard."

"I still think that my actual presence will be more of a detriment to them than a help. I *have* worked with assault victims in the past, and no amount of accent overcomes that kind of trauma," he told her as he sat back down. "Some people insist on being there for the interviews themselves, but I am not one of them. Additionally, based on the statements you got, I think this is the order in which you should talk to them. Not in his order. In the order of the ones that need the most reassurance."

She took his list and frowned at it. "You have the one that couldn't stop crying as the second to last."

"Yes, but her reaction is normal. The first name on the list was in shock when she spoke to you. Her reaction is unpredictable at this point. The others had a level of detachment that suggested they were on heavy medication as well. The clearest, most open and honest ones—in terms of reaction, I am not accusing anyone of lying—were the last two."

Persephone looked at him. "If you can get all that from the interviews, why the hell am I even going? Other than being the right gender?"

"I am not here to take over your case. I am trying to make this easier—not just on you but also on them. Everything I've said is... a suggestion, nothing more. I am simply... an adviser, and I in no way envy you your position."

She studied him for a moment, ignoring her mother as she brought them each a plate of food. The leopard and his gender were excuses that *he* was hiding behind. He was unwilling to talk to any of those women. He defended a homeless man but was unable to talk to a woman that had been raped? What kind of a double standard was that?

He looked down at his plate and picked up his fork with reluctance. Persephone started on her eggs. "No appetite?"

"Bit nauseous, actually. I... I took a bad knock to the head a few years back and have been somewhat prone to migraines since then," he admitted, closing his eyes for a moment. She watched him, wondering if this was another excuse or another part of the puzzle, the case he wouldn't talk about.

"Car accident?"

He shook his head, just a very slight movement that she almost missed. "Suspect. Whacked me right on the back of the head with his weapon of choice. A shovel. Reinforced steel, I believe it was. Yes, Katya, I have a headache, but you didn't have to come rushing in. Go finish your food."

Chapter Five

"Randolph?"

He opened his eyes, slow and wary. "Reynolds?"

"You really been out all day?"

"Shamefully, yes, but as much as I tried to work through it, the reemergence of my breakfast convinced me that I would not win that battle," he admitted, easing himself up to where he could sit. He looked around the room. It was much darker now, but that could have been due to the sheets that had been hung over the shades to block out the light. He would have to thank Mrs. Reynolds for her thoughtfulness. "You have spoken to all six women then?"

The younger Reynolds nodded, sitting down on the other bed. More of her hair was coming loose now, and she was emotionally drained in addition to the physical concerns. He should not have sent her alone, but he did not know how he could have gone on those interviews. Katya, first of all, but if he'd tried to speak to them, it wouldn't have been their faces he saw or their voices he heard. No wonder he had a bloody migraine.

"It is your turn to rest."

She shot him a dirty look. "No, I need to discuss what BB found or didn't find. And sometime today, I have to face my supervisors and the mayor and explain how this went from bad to worse and someone died when they already think I should have caught this bastard."

"That's not a fair judgment. You barely have a partner, and it is almost ridiculous that I'm here and not the FBI's team. Where is their task force? Where is their support?" Randolph demanded, wincing. His headache was not gone. If he pushed things, he'd get it back in full force. "Bloody morons. I'd like to see them do better."

She smiled a little. "We both know they couldn't."

"Exactly. Stay there. I will get a glass of water and take another pill, and we can discuss what you learned."

She nodded, fighting a yawn, and he turned to Katya, nudging the leopard over to do what she did best. He left the room, descending the stairs with a slow, careful pace, and crossing over into the kitchen. He went to the cupboard and took out a glass to fill with water.

"You don't look any better than when you laid down."

"Not much, that's true," he agreed, looking over at Mrs. Reynolds as he took a slow sip of his water. "However, your daughter is probably worse."

Lillian shook her head. "That girl..."

"I think if I stay down here for a few minutes more, she'll fall asleep on the bed there, and so I'm going to attempt to ensure that happens. Katya should help with that. Would you happen to know if she usually carries her phone on her, or is it something she has a habit of leaving elsewhere? Car? Table?"

"It's on her, and you will get an earful for taking it if you even dare to do it."

"I'm not letting those idiots wake her and waste her time. They can put that other idiot up in front of the press if they want or demand answers from him, but his incompetence is hardly worth encouraging."

Lillian studied him for a moment. "You are a strange man, Mr. Randolph. And I am not just saying that because you have a leopard."

He gave a slight shrug, continuing to drink his water. He figured he'd wait until the glass was empty at least, then refill it, and after that, he would go back up and get her phone. Then he would find Batscher's number, call him and find out what he'd learned of the man Katya had picked out, and keep the hounds at bay until Reynolds got at least a couple hours worth of rest. She couldn't afford to push herself further. If she made the kind of mistake he had—well, the situation would end far worse than it had for him, but it was bad enough what he'd been forced to witness.

Besides, she had notes somewhere on the questions he'd wanted her to ask, and he could read them over as well. He finished the glass and returned to the sink, filling it back up again before he started up the stairs. Katya greeted him at the door, and he smiled as he saw that Reynolds had, in fact, fallen asleep.

"Good girl," he told Katya, petting her head again.

"That was low, Randolph."

"Good lord, woman! Don't do that," he practically yelped, almost jumping off the couch at the sound of her voice. Persephone frowned. Someone was more than a little tightly wound. He sat down again and put a hand to his head. She could see that the migraine was not gone. His tendency toward ignoring his own body's complaints was no better than hers. "Do you ever sleep more than four hours?"

"Not usually," she admitted. "And I doubt you do when you're not being brought down by a migraine."

He shook his head. "Actually, as long as I manage to forget there's a leopard staring at me, I generally do rather well. However, I have never been particularly good at traveling and sleeping on the road never agreed with me regardless of the assignment."

Persephone sat down next to him. "If your head is bothering you so much, you should go back to bed. No one's forcing you to work through it, and it may as well be my shift now."

"No, I'm close to something here. Oh, and Batscher has the man with the leopard bite in custody at the moment. He thinks he's got his man, despite my efforts to convince him otherwise. I told him if he wished to go down this route he was on his own."

"You're going to let him fall on his face?"

"He is no friend of mine, and if he is not willing to step back and look at the situation properly, I am not going to intervene to save him from his own stupidity."

"What makes BB so convinced? He didn't think much of your leopard's id earlier."

Randolph set down his pen and leaned back, closing his eyes. "Something about newspaper clippings following the case. I tried to remind him that almost everyone in this town is bound to be following this case, but he did not want to hear it. My leopard bit the man, so this is good enough for Batscher and should be good enough for me."

"Tell me what you're really thinking. That theory you've been holding back."

Randolph opened his eyes again. "The woman is your sister."

Persephone shook her head. "What, because she fit his victim profile ten years ago? So did dozens of other women. Why her? That picture on the wall? She's long since moved on from here. She actually works overseas. She's married. Has three kids. The perfect, ideal life according to my mother. And while Sarah was always popular—her nickname is Sunny—I can't see anyone getting this warped over her."

"You asked. I answered. I told you that it was a waste of time.

Even if I could prove it, and I can't, I doubt your sister would remember the man. If the incident happened at all," Randolph said, and then he frowned. "Sunny? And you—"

"Ice Queen. Or White Witch. Take your pick," Persephone agreed, looking over at him. "I want to go talk to the guy your leopard bit. You going back to bed or coming with me? Oh, and give me back my damn phone."

Randolph handed it over to her. She took it and looked at him. "I think you should stay here. And I think the leopard would take my side."

"I should tell you what I got from your notes."

"You raided my notes, too? What the hell is wrong with you?"

"Do you really have to yell right now?" he asked, touching his head. "I am trying to be helpful here, and I can't do that with you shouting at me. Yes, I took your notes. I shouldn't have made you go on your own, but I—The point is that I have a few things we can discuss now that may help."

"I don't get you, Randolph. You're willing to push yourself pretty damn far for this case, but then you shy away from it at the same time."

He shrugged. "I never said I worked in anything close to a linear manner. I'm going to grab another pill and my coat, and then we can go."

Persephone looked over at the leopard. "Well? You think he should go? Because you're the one that can make him stay."

Katya jumped up on the couch and put herself in Randolph's lap. Persephone smiled at him, and he glared at the leopard. "Traitor."

"Where the hell have you been?"

"Let's see... I spoke to our six living victims and narcotics about the drugs and our homeless man who found the body. And what did you do today, BB? Bring in the wrong man? Nice. Excellent work. You deserve a promotion," Persephone snapped, moving past him into the interrogation room. She picked up the file on the table and looked at the kid. "What were you doing up on that roof?"

"I just wanted to get a good look. That's it. I've been saying that all along, but that bozo won't listen. Keeps telling me I can get a lawyer and all that, but I ain't got nothing to hide. I'm gonna sue your department for all its worth because I got bit by a damn leopard, but I didn't do anything to any of those girls."

"And I suppose you'd be willing to give us DNA to test against our evidence?"

"Yeah," the punk said, leaning into her face. She didn't back down. He could use a breath mint, though, and he reeked of stale cigarettes. "'Cause I ain't got nothing to hide, Frosty. I was just enjoying the view."

"Of a dead woman?"

"Well..."

She reached into the folder and took out the clippings that BB had bagged as evidence. "Talk to me about this. Since you've got nothing to hide and all."

"It was news, okay? It was just... news. I was curious. That's it."

She shook her head. "Where's the camera?"

"What?"

"You weren't up there just to look. Did you take the pictures on your phone, or is there a separate camera? BB, you have his phone?"

The other detective came into the room, setting the phone on the table. "You want to explain this email to the newspapers offering them pictures of a dead woman?"

"Freedom of the press, yo. Ever heard of that?"

"Listen to me very carefully," Persephone began, walking around behind him and shoving him back down in his chair. He cried out when the sore from his leopard bite hit the hard plastic. "This? It's obstruction now. You're wasting my time. You're wasting Batscher's time. It still looks pretty bad for you. You really want the press to get your name and start putting it out there that you're a rapist and a murderer? All it takes is one article to ruin the rest of your life. How long have you been following this thing? How many of the other crime scenes have you been to? How many of those women did you leave lying there helpless while you photographed them for your own sick amusement?"

"You really are a witch, aren't you, Frosty?" the kid leaned back in his chair. "Your bad cop act don't scare me none."

She gave him a slight smile. "You are all talk, aren't you? How would you like it if I let the leopard in to come say hello? She really likes watching from the other side of the glass. Drools all over it. And then when she gets in here..."

The punk paled. He shook his head. "Okay, okay. All I did was take some pictures. I gave them to a few people, tried to sell them to the papers and stuff, but they kept jerking me around. I thought I hit it big when I got the dead one because they'd want to see that, right? I noticed you ain't told them what he did to her face or how she died or nothin' so why wouldn't they pay for these, huh?"

She shook her head, angry enough to smack him. "What about the man who left them behind? You ever see him?"

"Some guy in a coat and hat. Nothing special about him."

"The man raped seven women and killed one of them, but you didn't think he was worth paying attention to? What the hell is wrong with you?"

The kid shrugged. "So what? He was just a dude."

"Just a dude," Persephone repeated. "Oh, hell, I am getting that damn leopard."

"Easy now, Reynolds. No need for that," BB began, sitting down and trying to take over as good cop. She shook her head and walked out of the room, leaning against the wall. She didn't believe this. She knew it wouldn't stick, but she wanted that damn kid as an accessory after the fact. He sat there and let that man get away with it. How did that even happen? What twisted that kid up so that he could be okay with that? So that he didn't care about the hell those women had been through?

She'd sat there with them, made them go over the worst moment of their lives, and promised them she'd find the man that did this, and that kid in there let him walk away. More than once. She didn't understand. She wanted to scream or break things—break that damn smug kid.

She had half a mind to call Randolph, make sure he had that leopard down here when the little bastard was moved to holding. It was the least she should do to him.

Chapter Six

"Here."

"You really ditch that headache already?"

"It's duller now," Randolph told her, almost forcing the drink
on her. She took it and sipped from it, looking at him in surprise. He
shrugged. "I never said it was coffee."

She took a deep breath and shook her head. "Thought you'd
be above the tea thing. You said you were British in name only,
remember? Well, that and accent and education."

"You were listening."

"I do that. Occupational hazard. Not as bad as you, though," she
said, taking the lid off the cup and reaching in for the bag. She dunked
it in and out for a few minutes. "I told myself I'm not allowed to see
the newspapers today. If I start to look, stop me."

"Deal," he agreed, sitting down next to her. "What happened with
Bite Boy?"

"Bite Boy?"

"I didn't get a name, so I'm improvising. You liked it, though. I
saw that bit of a smile when I said it," Randolph told her, and then she
ducked her head, fighting laughter. He smiled back at her, reaching

over to pet Katya's head for a moment before the leopard went over to put her head on Reynolds' lap. The detective looked down at the cat and sighed.

"He saw our guy. Didn't pay any attention to him. Just wanted to photograph the women he left behind. They were hurt and vulnerable, and all that bastard did was exploit them further."

Randolph cursed, leaning back in his chair. Katya lifted her head, but he waved her back down. Reynolds needed the leopard more at the moment.

"What makes a person think that's okay? He's almost worse than the damn rapist."

"I can't really speak to what kind of morality Bite Boy was raised with. Can't say what might have defined him, but clearly he lacks real respect for women and quite possibly for human life in general. Chances are he grew up with a woman who didn't respect herself or a man who instilled in him that they were worthless. Then again, he could have come from a warm, loving home and just decided he didn't give a damn. I'm not going to start in on debating nature versus nurture. That's dangerous ground for a profiler. Or for the world in general. Like blaming the murders committed by those teenagers at Columbine on their parents and the authorities instead of the boys themselves. Don't forget—nature, nurture, or any lack thereof—that doesn't mean that free will went out the window. I grew up without a father. Doesn't make me a criminal, didn't make me hate all authority figures, and while I respect my mother, I am also not that charming term—not a 'Mama's boy.'"

"Just like not all people who suffer abuse go on to abuse someone else," she agreed, drinking more of the tea. "I might not think much of BB half the time, but he's a cop after going through some really crappy stuff growing up. There is a choice. You're right."

"Not always," Randolph disagreed. "You need a bit longer or should we press on with what I wanted to discuss last night?"

"You needed to ditch the damn migraine, and if you'd been here, that would *not* have helped anything."

"I suppose not. I would have let Katya bite him again."

Reynolds laughed. "I can't imagine that tasted pleasant."

"Doubt it. Look at her expression. She did not think much of that one, either."

Reynolds looked down. "I don't know. I haven't quite mastered reading her expressions like you."

"Just takes a bit of practice."

"Yeah. Okay, tell me what you got from those interviews. All I got was the sense of a lot of pain and misery and a few *what the hell kind of a question is that* looks, so you can fill me in on the rest of it, yes?"

"A few things," he agreed. It still was not much. "We are looking for a man who most likely owns his own home somehow. One with a basement."

She frowned. "How did you come up with that one?"

"The combination of the fact that no one sees him coming or going. No one hears their screams despite the fact that more than one of them said they heard their voice echoing off the walls. The acoustics they describe make me think basement, as does the fact that they all remember cold. No one described air flowing, but they had chills—and not just because of what he was—Then there's the lack of light. He grabs them sometimes in the middle of the day and dumps them by the night, meaning he's ensured a place with minimal light where he—He doesn't restrain them. Yes, they're drugged, but I believe the drugs are mostly about them not seeing him, not being able to fight him because he needs that illusion that this is... voluntary even if it's the furthest thing from it. Still, he knows that they couldn't find their way out. Again, a basement with the only access being from inside the house. Possibly one that was illegally finished and has no building permits for any of the work done down there."

Reynolds took that in. "Okay, yes, sounds like a basement. Do you realize you can't even say what he's doing?"

Randolph sighed. "Can you picture all of this in your head?"

"To a frightening degree."

"Amplify that by ten and you have the world of a profiler. I... see both sides of it. And I sometimes stumble over the actual events.

Doesn't matter what I'm looking at. I see way too much."

"Why keep doing it, then? Even with a leopard, there have to be better ways to make money."

"It's not about the money."

Of course not. It was personal. It was hard to say just how personal it was with Randolph. She knew he'd already figured her out, but she hadn't gotten as far with him. She didn't have his training or statistics, and she didn't want them. Maybe that was selfish of her, but she could see what it did to him. She didn't need to go there. She looked down at the leopard, his therapy cat, and wondered if he had any idea how much *he* needed Katya. Probably not.

"So we know he owns his own house and he's set it up to do this. What else have we got?" Persephone asked, nudging Katya out of her lap as she rose, going over to the dry erase board and picking up the marker. She wrote down the few things they knew about their man—the house, the description Bite Boy had given them, the dark hair, the rejection, and the sundress. She stepped back and looked at Randolph. "Cars."

"Hmm?"

"He has to have more than one or access to them because no one from the abduction sites reported the same kind of car, we got nothing with the surveillance videos or traffic cameras... A few similar types of car, but that doesn't mean much."

"So he has a couple of unremarkable cars he switches between," Randolph agreed. "I have a bit of a theory to put forth, but bear in mind that it is a theory, please."

She looked at him. "What?"

"It goes with the house ownership. I think he may have recently inherited it from a female relative—mother or grandmother, possibly aunt—who was... rather an overwhelming presence in his life."

"Her loss triggering the start of the rapes?"

"Possibly. But if he did inherit this home he may also have inherited a vehicle or two as well."

Persephone wrote down inheritance and put a question mark after it. Randolph's theory fit, made sense, but they didn't have anything to prove it with, either. She stood back and studied the board. "Not enough yet."

"Getting closer," he said, and she set down the marker, returning to her desk. She sat down and reached for her tea, looking up as BB came into the room with a loud grunt.

"Finished with Bite Boy then?"

BB snorted. "Bite Boy?"

"Mine, actually. I don't remember the name of the individual in question, and it did get a smile and a bit of laughter out of her as well as you," Randolph explained. He smiled down at the leopard. "Yes, yes, love, I know you're very proud of your work. You are a very smart leopard."

Persephone sipped from her tea and looked at Batscher. "You sending him over to county?"

BB nodded. "Yeah. He'll be on his way soon. Kid's a freaking *mess.* Makes my skin crawl. You're lucky you walked when you did."

"Had to. Would have done something I regretted," Persephone said. She looked at the leopard. "You want to say hello to your friend before he leaves?"

Katya bared her teeth. Randolph looked at her. "Okay, not your friend. Still, you want to play, don't you? Play statue, maybe?"

The leopard licked his hand and then padded over to sit right in the middle of the hallway. She just sat, didn't seem to blink or even breathe. BB let out a whistle. "That's creepy."

"Sometimes I use that when I need to use the restroom," Randolph admitted. "She won't leave until I tell her to—that's the game—but she doesn't always like to play it."

"It's perfect for this," Persephone agreed, watching the uniforms lead the kid close. He started to panic at the sight of the leopard, trying to climb the walls or anything he could to get away from her. Katya just sat, still like a statue, acting like she didn't see what the kid was doing. One of the uniforms tried to budge her, but she didn't move, so they went around, the kid's eyes never leaving the cat.

Just as they were at the door, Randolph spoke. "Katya."

The leopard gave up the statue routine, running over to his side and getting another scream out of the kid as she did. BB doubled over at his desk, unable to stop laughing. Persephone couldn't help a grim smile. Randolph patted the leopard's head. "Good girl."

"I need another one of these. Or a coffee. Or both," Reynolds muttered as she finished her tea. She dropped the empty cup into the trash by her desk and looked over at the board again. "And someone deserves a reward for that performance, don't you?"

Katya leaned into the woman's hand and purred. Randolph was going to have to have a long talk with his leopard. He could see that she was becoming rather attached to Reynolds, even extending a bit of the same protectiveness she had for him to the detective, but this was temporary. He looked at the cat. "You don't get to keep her."

"I am not trying to steal your leopard."

Randolph did not correct her assumption. He did not think she would like knowing he was talking to the cat. The leopard started to circle around Reynolds, and he shook his head. If that was how the leopard really felt, she'd have to make up her mind. Randolph would have to go where he was needed, and so Katya would have to make a choice.

"I agree, though. Let us get some sustenance and then we can go from there. Have you heard from the ballistics lab? Do we have the make and model of the gun yet? Can we start tracking down registered owners?"

"Bring me back something, and I'll talk to the lab, even start running the names," BB said, and Reynolds gave him a look. He shrugged. "Gotta make up for yesterday, right?"

"Sure," she said. She grabbed her suit jacket and pulled it on as she headed for the door. Randolph sighed. She shouldn't bother with that. Judging from the already warm morning he'd noticed on his way to the station, they would all be looking to get rid of their layers by the end of the day. "What?"

He turned to Reynolds. So she'd caught that last thought. "The day will be warm."

"More women in sundresses?" She shook her head, moving toward the door. "You think it's worth releasing something to the press to tell the women here not to wear sundresses? Would that even make a difference?"

He considered for a moment. "We do have a good idea of the type that he's looking for, and yes, warning them is probably a good idea.

Perhaps a press conference this afternoon is... necessary."

She looked out at the sun. "BB, need you to take the speech making."

"You're the lead on this thing."

"Well, until someone learns to schedule these things indoors and out of the sun, it's going to have to be you," she said, pulling on her jacket, trying to make it cover her hands. "Gonna need the damn hat and the gloves."

Randolph followed her out of the station, Katya right behind them. "You might try walking in my shadow—not in the figurative sense, that is not what I'm getting at—but it is a limited amount of shade that might help if the sun's effects are so strong."

"I might end up being the red queen if I'm not careful. And then I get itchy and can't work because I can't think," she said, going to the trunk of her car and pulling out a wide brim hat, putting it on her head. "You can laugh if you want. They usually do. I look like... a beekeeper or something."

"Hardly," he disagreed as she reached in for a bottle of heavy duty sunblock. "You could turn it into another theme look, as you did with the cream suit you wore the other day."

"Your observation about the white witch aside, I don't actually enjoy being a spectacle because of a couple of recessive genes that should never have managed to combine for... this."

"You can embrace it, or you can fight it. I tried fighting the leopard. Look where it got me."

She smiled a little, and he took her sunglasses out of her pocket, handing them to her. She sighed. "Could have sworn I checked that pocket earlier."

He shrugged. "Does wearing a thin fabric or something... see-through—I can't remember what they call that stuff—ever work? Or do you burn if you're at all exposed, even with the fabric over it?"

"Why do you care?"

"Because from what little I've experienced in it, that building has nothing in the way of air conditioning, and I don't think it's right for you to have to deal with heat exhaustion on top of everything else."

"I stick to the dress code."

"Which you have every right to be the exception to," he insisted. "You need to be able to work. You gain nothing by keeping quiet about unjust conditions. This isn't something you have to put up with to do your job. If they won't fix the air conditioning, then they have to accept your modifications to the dress code."

"We all suck it up and do our jobs. I don't need or want special treatment. The guys wear suits, too. And I don't need more ice queen comments or ones about me melting or anything like that."

He looked over at Katya, trying to rein in a few choice comments he might have made and an urge to do something far stupider. "You are working with a shrink who has a leopard, remember? How could your reputation possibly get any lower?"

Reynolds laughed. "Fine. You win. We'll stop by my place and get a different shirt, too. And you need to change as well. That is the same suit you were wearing when we met, isn't it?"

He looked down. He'd completely lost track. "Maybe."

"You're not joining me in throwing out the dress code?" Persephone asked, studying Randolph for a moment after he emerged from the shower. His hair was wet and sticking to his forehead, but he still had most of a suit on, missing only the tie and jacket.

"I didn't pack a lot of variety in my clothes. In deference, though, I am not going with the tie," he answered, smiling a little. He looked at the cup in her hands. "There another one of those for me?"

She nodded, pointing to the counter. He picked up the cup and took a sip, shaking his head as he watched the leopard eat for a moment. "Never going to get used to that, honestly. Doesn't help when I go back to a few other cases that I've worked. Still... I suppose we need to get back to Batscher and give him the food and coffee we promised."

"He'll live, and I don't think we should interrupt Katya at the moment."

"True." Randolph moved over and sat down on the other chair. She only had the two in her apartment, and she didn't need the second one. She'd cleaned it off when she got here, though, wincing a little when she realized just how long it had been since she'd had a chance to do anything more than walk through here. It was a disaster area, and she didn't want to know what his shrink mind was coming up with as he looked around.

"I... haven't been home in a while."

"Work comes before a clean house. We know that well, don't we, Katya?" Randolph asked, getting a look from the leopard. He rolled his eyes. "You chased off the cleaning lady. That was *not* my fault. That was all you. You see, we had someone who did that for us for a while, but Katya spooked her. She was being friendly, really, but the screams echoed down the street and very nearly got us evicted."

Persephone laughed. He shrugged, drinking from his cup. She was finding his unbuttoned collar very distracting at the moment, though she didn't know why. She cleared her throat, turning back to the leopard. "I don't know how you can afford to feed her and keep an apartment."

"I am going to have to make sure that I factor in the cost of her food when I tell people what my services will cost, but so far we have managed to make it work, haven't we?"

Katya didn't look up from her food. He rolled his eyes, finishing off his coffee. "There's a pot in the kitchen?"

"Yes."

"Will you get angry if I ask you a personal question?"

"That depends. We already argued about my clothes, and I believe you've even seen some of my underwear, so I'm not sure where the line is anymore," she admitted, wishing she'd taken him back to her mother's instead of letting him set foot in her mess of an apartment.

He nodded, a bit uncomfortable. "Actually... It was about the four hours of sleep."

"What about it?"

He brought the pot over to her and poured some into the cup in her hands. "It's a cycle—a habit—that you can't break. Has been since your father died and you got that call in the middle of the night, hasn't it?"

"I hate you. How do you even—how can you—It doesn't matter. Not everything in my life is about my father's death."

"No, but the sleep thing is, and it is why you became a cop," Randolph said as he sat back down. She lifted the cup to her lips, and he studied his, lost in thought. "You wake suddenly, always expecting that call, no matter when it is or how long you've been asleep. And this job doesn't help—it just reenforces the behavior when you get the call late at night."

She set her cup down. "He owned a convenience store. Worked there every day of our lives. After my sister left for college, he swore he'd stop working the night shift. He wasn't even supposed to be there. I don't know why he was. I just know I woke up to the phone. It was one of the kids that worked there, freaked out, told me my father was dead, and then a policeman took the phone away from him and tried to explain the whole thing in much gentler way, but it was kind of... too late for that. I had to wake my mother, and we went down there and... And I swore I would do my part to make sure that no one else got that kind of a call. Ever."

"You can't stop them all."

"I know that," she agreed, reaching for the coffee again. "And I know today or maybe tomorrow I will have to go and tell a family that their daughter or sister or wife is dead, and it never gets any easier. Still, no one should have to sit there and wonder why eighty-seven dollars is worth a man's life."

"The robber was never caught."

"No, and I saw the tapes. My father cooperated. The safe was locked, nothing he could do about that, and he gave him everything in the till, and that bastard still shot him," Persephone shook her head in frustration. "I can't believe I let you bring that up again."

"Occupational hazard," Randolph whispered. "I make connections and have a tendency just to... blurt them out."

"You asked for permission this time."

"Not for all of it."

Persephone was trying to figure out what to say to that, but then Katya came up to her, putting a paw on her thigh. "Um, cat, no offense, but I know where you've just been and what you were doing, and it's not much comfort at the moment."

Katya dropped down and curled up by her feet, purring. Randolph forced a smile. "She is done eating, at least, so when you're ready, we can go back. As you said, we should see if there's been any progress made on identifying our latest victim."

Persephone nodded. "Let's go."

"Nothing yet. Our victim has never been in the system for any reason, and no one has reported her missing yet," Reynolds said, putting the phone back down on the cradle, looking over at her board again. She shook her head. "I do not know how this is even possible. How can she slip through the cracks like that?"

"She could have been a passing motorist. This city does have two state highways running through it. Not an interstate, but there is a fair amount of traffic that goes through here daily. She could have stopped for lunch or gas. Or she doesn't have family nearby to realize she's gone."

Reynolds sighed, shaking her head. She rose and went to the board, adding the gun to the list and backing away again. "Where is that list BB gave us?"

Randolph stood up and gave it to her. She looked at it and then at him. "Anything you've got that can narrow this down for us?"

"Nothing new," Randolph admitted. He rubbed the back of his neck. His headache was coming back, but he actually wanted to get his hands on a list the names of men in her sister's classes and cross-reference them with gun registrations and recent deaths. It was a tenuous connection at best, but he kept going back to that picture that had caught his eye the minute he walked into her mother's house, and he couldn't shake it. Something was there. "Unless you want to follow through with my other theory."

"About my sister, you mean? It could have been anyone—if that woman exists."

"You said you wanted a way to narrow it down. If you connected the registration and the inheritance and the class your sister was in, that's narrow, isn't it?"

Reynolds nodded with reluctance, rubbing her arms. The lighter fabric suited her, and the tunic's long sleeves managed to cover most of her hands. "It might be, but we're still grabbing a woman at random. That's not going to stand up in court, and it won't get us the warrant we'd need to make the connection."

"Could get us a name to talk to."

"And then what? Spook him? Push him to take another woman?"

"It would be his right to refuse the ballistics test, but... It would be suspicious. And... if he's an amateur as far as guns go, he could easily have injured himself on the slide when he shot her. That would be another possible sign."

She let out a breath. "Fine. We'll get the lists and compare them. It can't hurt anything. It's not like we have much else to go on, and so far your instincts have been rather good."

"I am not infallible, though. I have been wrong several times in the past."

"I didn't think you were perfect," she said, turning back to her desk and sitting down again. She shook her mouse, waking up her computer. "Your headache is back, isn't it?"

He sat in the other chair. "It's not bad yet."

"Don't listen to him; that's what he always says."

Katya gave a low growl. Randolph shook his head as he turned around. "What are you doing here, Marcie?"

The other man put a bottle down on the desk. "You know better than to travel without them. And, what, you thought I wouldn't notice that your case—"

"My case. My job. I do not need you looking over my shoulder,"

Randolph snapped, getting to his feet. "You do not need to babysit me. I can handle this."

"Yeah. Clearly."

Marciano ignored him. He turned to Reynolds. "How many headaches has he had? Is he jumping at shadows yet?"

"Marcie, you may think you're acting like a friend, but this is unacceptable. This is—I am fine. If it was a problem, the leopard or Reynolds would have dealt with it, and I do not need you checking up on me like I'm a child. I've handled dozens of cases—"

"Not like this and you know it. The last time one of these took this turn—"

"I got whacked over the head with a shovel. I haven't forgotten."

Randolph yanked the pills off the desk and headed for the door, the leopard at his side. Persephone stood up and faced the man still standing there. She knew who he was—Angie had pictures of all of her family and shared them even with people who didn't want to see them—but the name "Marcie" would have been enough if she hadn't. "What the hell was that? Are you really just here for him or are the feds moving in on my case?"

"Just for him," Marciano said, leaning against her desk. She gave him a look, and he sighed. "Randolph didn't tell you, did he?"

"About the shovel? Yes, he did, at least as far it's the cause of his migraines. He had one yesterday. Took him out for the better part of the day, but he forced himself to work through it this morning. What are those pills, and what made you come here?"

"The murder."

She let out a breath. "You don't think my department can handle this?"

"Has nothing to do with you, Reynolds. Angie likes you. She thinks you're good at what you do. It's him. His past."

Persephone nodded. She knew there was something there, had seen a few things that didn't add up, but nothing that meant that his friend had to show up here and check on him. "What, exactly? What is it that worries you so much? You said... when the last case took this turn, and by that you mean... the murder, right? Hasn't he worked dozens of them? That's how he got the leopard, isn't it? Working a murder?"

"It's the last time he worked a serial rapist's case."

She folded her arms over her chest. She wasn't liking where this was going, and she had a feeling she'd like it even less as it went on. "You're the one that arranged this. If he can't handle cases like this, why the hell did you do that?"

"He's avoided them for a while now, but the leopard makes things difficult for him. He didn't have much of a choice, and he needs this job. He also... shouldn't be working it. The last time he worked a case like this, when the man started killing... It went to hell. Fast."

"Explain. Fast."

Marciano almost laughed. The situation didn't allow for it, though. "You know how it is. We rotate through multiple cases. It's never just one. Randolph had the guy pinned down, created a profile—an accurate one, fit the bastard to a tee—and he moved on, focusing on the newer case while the local authorities were supposed to be arresting the man he'd found. They couldn't find him because the freak had started stalking Randolph. Got it in his head that a man who understood him that well had to be a part of the next one or it wouldn't be complete. So, yes, Randolph got whacked over the head with a shovel. And the killer made him watch all of it."

Persephone winced. Now all of the little things added up, and she really didn't like the picture. "And then what?"

"Randolph ended up taking the guy out. We don't know all the details—he's never been able to give them. Between the concussion and the trauma, he doesn't even know."

Persephone let out a breath. "I don't understand. Why let him take this case then? It was bound to bring up all of that."

"He can't get that woman's voice out of his head. If he stops working, he feels like he's failing her all over again. The only way to keep that guilt from overwhelming him is to keeping doing this job no matter how much it costs him. When the leopard got him fired, I went looking for something to keep him going. This was the first thing, and I had to weigh it against the damage it could do versus what would happen if he *didn't* have something to work on."

Persephone shook her head. "He shouldn't be here, and you know that. Hell, even the leopard knows that. If you'd told me about this upfront, I never would have let him come."

"He won't quit. Not now."

"I think that the leopard should bite you now. What—You never should have let him do this. He should not have been exposed to any of it."

"Has he helped?"

"Yes," she had to admit. She knew he'd done a lot to help them already. "But if this case takes him, is it really worth it?"

Chapter Seven

"He told you."

Reynolds nodded as she sat down next to him. Katya moved, draping herself on top of their feet, and Randolph frowned at her even as she gave him that blank stare like she had no idea why he was questioning her. He didn't understand.

"You should have told me."

"It doesn't affect this. It's in the past, and he had no right to meddle in—"

"You couldn't interview them. You nearly had a panic attack in that alley. And your head is killing you. Don't say it doesn't matter. It does. This is not a small thing, Randolph. It isn't going away, either. The longer you work this case, the harder it's going to get," she told him, and he closed his eyes, hating the images that filled his head when he did.

"Don't ask me to stop, Reynolds. Not with another monster like him out there. She'll just get louder and louder until that's all I hear," Randolph whispered, lowering his head. He felt the detective's hand on his back and looked at her. It was some small mercy that she was so distinctive—the white witch—impossible to mistake for anyone other than herself. "Can't get that look out of my head, the one where she begged me to help her, and there was nothing I could do. This—this I can do. This I *have* to do."

"Even if it kills you?"

"You can't back away any more than I can, you know that," he said, tempted to take hold of some of her hair. He knew her presence, like Katya's, was a comfort in of itself, and her hand on his back was another connection, but he wanted to take it further. He did not.

Reynolds reached for the bottle. "And these?"

"Supposed to help prevent the migraines. Doesn't work."

"Not if you don't take them."

He almost smiled at that. She did have a point there, but he did not wish to discuss the poor state of his finances at the moment. Staying on here had very little to do with the money—though he could not deny that he needed it, needed to start building a reputation as a consultant if he was going to continue to support himself—but none of that was why he *had* to do this.

"If I let you stay, I want your promise that you'll tell me everything—no holding back theories no matter how far-fetched or how I react to them, no covering up reactions to something from this case because of the past, no lying about your headaches. If it's bad, I want you backing off and giving yourself time to cope with it."

"Does that mean you'll try to sleep more than you have been?"

She shrugged. "I suppose that's a fair enough trade. You know I don't understand all of what you do or even like it that much, but I can admit you're good at it. Too good to let this thing take you down with it."

"It's always easier to see someone else's problems, to point them out and even attempt to fix them," he admitted. He reached to run his fingers through the fur of the leopard holding down his feet. "I think it has become a defense mechanism of sorts—pointing out something about the other person to make sure the focus stays off of me. I have used it against you—I'm not proud of it—but some of the times I made observations about your father were deliberate attempts to push you away from... this."

Reynolds nodded. "I know."

Randolph looked at her. "Why Persephone?"

She gave him a slight smile. "My parents thought I needed a special name to go with the special looks. Neither of them were all that into classic literature or anything—not sure they'd even read up on the particular myth they got the name from. They just liked the way it sounded. Why psychology?"

"The need to understand the way the human mind worked. Not brain surgery... morality and thought process and how a man could lead such a convincing double life. My mother never knew herself as the other woman until I came along, you see. They dated, they moved in together, and there was discussion of marriage, everything seemed like a normal relationship until a certain test. I never knew him, so psychology seemed like a way to understand him."

"And do you understand him, then? Do you know why he did it?"

"He was a selfish wanker," Randolph answered, and she laughed. "Years of schooling, and that is all I figured out. About him, at least, but then there is very little worth knowing there."

She shrugged. "You didn't say you agreed to the terms."

Randolph nodded. "Yes. I agree to the terms. We should go inside before you get burned for my sake."

She reached up. "I forgot the hat."

"And the sunglasses," he pointed out. She sighed. He looked at her. "You were that worried about me? Or... the case?"

"The leopard."

"I don't remember inviting you to help yourself to anything, Marciano," Persephone said as she and Randolph returned to her desk. She folded her arms over her chest, and then Katya went over and put her paws on Marciano's legs, staring him down. Randolph started laughing, and Persephone frowned as Marciano gave the leopard a look and then turned to his friend.

"This what I think it is?"

"The leopard likes the lady. Don't make her angry," Randolph advised, stealing the chair from the other desk. "You could get in trouble for butting in where you haven't been asked, you know."

Marciano snorted. "Like this shouldn't be something a team is working on. Where is the team? Here? You, her, and the leopard?"

"And an idiot she calls BB," Randolph added. Persephone gave him a look. He shrugged. "I do not think very highly of Batscher, I have to say. He has done little to improve my opinion, but then I have not worked with him for long, either. Marcie, go home. The wife barely sees you as it is."

"Can't go without seeing Angie, and you know that my wife understands the job. Hell, you worked with her more than I did. And lay off the Marcie crap. You know how I feel about that," Marciano countered. He started scratching around the leopard's ears, and Katya gave out a low, rumbling purr. Persephone glanced in Randolph's direction.

He shook his head. "Traitor."

Katya looked back at him, pretending to be innocent, and he rolled his eyes. Persephone would almost have been able to forget that he'd stormed out of here and almost broken down outside, but she was aware of what this really was. Randolph was pretending he was fine, and his friend was letting him. Even the leopard was going along with it at the moment. Persephone shook her head and went over to pick up her hat and sunglasses.

"Going somewhere?"

"Back to the beginning. Want to see if there's anything there I missed like at the supermarket."

"You no longer want to narrow down the gun list?"

She put the hat on and reached around the leopard for her keys. "You really think he's using a registered gun? I doubt it. And your theory about the rest of it... I still can't accept that. Besides, this—I feel cooped up in here, and it's not helping. I need to think."

"You could try sleeping."

The way Randolph looked at her just then gave her the oddest thoughts that had nothing to do with sleep, and she shook her head. "I can't work on this basing the whole thing on the idea that my sister rejected him and he started doing this because of her... That's just a good way to make *me* shut down. So if you want to cross-reference all of that, do it. I can't. I'll go focus on what I *can* do."

"I can put in a call to the wife and have her run down the connection," Marciano offered. Persephone frowned. Randolph smiled, shaking his head a little. "Never call her a geek, but that woman can do amazing things with a keyboard. Amazing things with her hands, too. Ah, *amore...* Such a strange and wonderful thing, isn't it?"

"I really have no idea," Persephone told him. She put her sunglasses on and headed for the door.

⟡

"You said this was about her sister?" Marciano demanded with a wince. "What is wrong with you? You don't just tell a person that. Especially not *that* one."

"Her sister fits the victim profile perfectly. She does not."

Marcie shook his head. "You know that's not what I meant, Randolph. You said the leopard likes her, which is something considering how she usually reacts to the people you work with and even your building manager and cleaning lady... You made a new friend who puts up with the leopard, and you want to shove her away with a theory about her sister? How sure are you that there's a connection?"

Randolph sighed. He rose and paced for a moment. "Sometimes I have those moments—same as every other investigator—where I just *know* that there's something there. Goes against evidence or common sense, but it's there. And when I saw the picture of her family, that was the feeling I got. I strongly believe that this man knew her sister, that she was—and this is not to blame her or make her responsible for any of his actions—but she *was* his catalyst. This theory keeps building on itself. The inheritance—the domineering mother—she knew Sarah Reynolds, and she thought that girl was everything and every time he heard that, he broke a little more. He can't get to the Reynolds woman now because she's overseas, but his mother is finally gone, and the perfect woman is out of reach, so he's going after proxies. And yes, I know I have no proof, and I am not letting it get in the way of looking into other things. I suggested that we do the cross-checking when Reynolds—Persephone, that is—wanted a way to narrow down the gun registration. She has a point about the gun, though. This guy wouldn't use one that's in his name. It's also unlikely that he'd use one that was in his mother's name. Of course, that all assumes that that part of my earlier inferences is correct, that it's not just a crazy theory."

"I will run it down for you," Marciano said. "Still... This reminds me of when you were working that other case—the arson one—and came up with that wild theory about the local agent's uncle that very nearly got you kicked out of town."

"He *was* a pyromaniac who had set fires to abandoned buildings and did things while he watched them burn. He just wasn't the arsonist we were looking for. I'm not always right, and I'm the first to admit that. I know I can't... Nothing I do is exact—it gets backed up with evidence that makes it *seem* that way, and I have statistics that can almost act as proof, but it's all in how I interpret what I see."

"And now that she's not here to hear it, you can finally admit you're wondering if your judgment is being affected by the other case, by what happened before."

Randolph frowned, sitting down again, and Katya came over and tried to climb into his lap. "You're too big for that, love. Just sit there."

"Well?" Marciano prompted. "It's true, isn't it?"

"I was right about him escalating. I was right about the way he sees these women. I can help. I know I have to do this... I don't know if the conviction I got looking at the photo is anything or just... me grabbing at anything that might end this faster."

"Go find your friend. Walk through it with her again. I'll call you when I have something."

Randolph looked at him. "You're not here officially and—"

"Go. So what if someone else runs the search? It's an unlikely theory, isn't it?"

"And if I am right?"

"You said the sister was safe, remember?"

Persephone studied the lot again, shaking her head. This place was not where you'd expect a woman to go missing. It wasn't deserted enough. Maybe that was only in this back corner, where she'd parked

106

for no reason that Persephone could tell. It wasn't close enough to the large shops or the small strip of fast food restaurants and small stores that were nearby.

She sat down on the trunk of her car, fanning herself in the heat and trying to figure it out. She'd parked under the tree, but at that time of the morning, why worry about shade? The sun was barely out. Why park so damn far away?

She could call and ask, she supposed. That should settle the matter. Still, while she didn't have—or want—Randolph's job, something about this spot would not let her go. She studied it with a frown, distracted from her thoughts when the old Plymouth pulled in next to her car. She turned to see the leopard rolling down the window on the passenger side of the car before she jumped out. Persephone shook her head, watching the cat pad her way over to where she sat. She reached down to pet Katya as Randolph joined them.

"Didn't really believe you'd still be here."

"Going to have to ask her why the hell she parked here at five in the morning. The coffee joint is all the way at the end there—it has a drive-thru right over there—and the store is even further in the opposite direction. I could see wanting the shade of the tree, but at five in the morning?"

"You have half your answer already."

Persephone frowned. "What?"

"What are you doing?"

"Sitting on my car. Wait, you think she drove through the drive-thru, got her coffee and maybe a bagel or something and then parked here to eat? Why not go inside?"

"You ever sit in a coffee shop for a long time?"

"Fine, I take your point. If it's not the other customers in there, it's the machines themselves," she agreed. This was a lot quieter, a lot more peaceful. "Still, if that's why she was here, why does her statement say, 'I was getting in my car, and he grabbed me?' I can't believe I'm asking that. I don't want to say I—I do not believe she was lying about being raped. That is not what this is."

"No, but she may have lied about how he took her," Randolph said. He pointed behind Persephone. "There's a sidewalk there, not far from this car. He's walking down, she has no idea he spotted her earlier and parked his car where she wouldn't see it. He comes up like he's just walking along, minding his own business, he talks to her casually, and she might even have been enjoying the conversation, completely unaware of what he intended to do. So he gets closer, she starts to leave, he moves in with the drugs..."

"And she covers that part up so that people don't accuse her of encouraging him."

"Yes."

Despite the heat, Persephone shivered. "It is so wrong that she felt she had to hide that."

"Time to talk to her again, though. She can tell us more about that time before he grabbed her. What he spoke about, the sound of his voice. Accent or no accent. What his footsteps sounded like. Possibly even a look at him out of the corner of her eye."

Persephone shook her head. "I can understand why she did this, but it makes me so damn angry. We could have had a lot more to work with *weeks* ago if people didn't treat this kind of crime with that stigma. What is it about sex that makes everyone assume that any kind of discussion of it is really a lie? Or that someone would really *want* to lie about that happening to them against their will?"

"Fear."

"What?"

"Think about it. Some people twist sex into the reason humans lost paradise. When it comes right down to it, most of them are actually scared of it to some degree or other. Fear of it not being good, fear of being used, fear of falling in love or out of love, fears of infidelity or being caught in the act of infidelity, fear of creating offspring or getting a disease, fears from former abuse... Add in generations that weren't able to discuss it in any kind of healthy manner and the way that some people handle educating children about it—a stork instead of a biological process? That has gone out of practice, I know, but the point is still valid. We could start debating morality, or we could even explore how for many years people linked sexual desire—particularly in *women*—with madness. All that does, though, is give me another headache. It's ignorance and fear and almost always handled badly. Oh, and then we get television sensationalizing the whole thing—"

"Stop, please," Persephone interrupted, reaching up to take his hand away from his forehead. He looked at her. "You really can get lost in tangents, can't you?"

"Bad habit of mine, yes." Katya walked over and bumped him, and he leaned down to pet her. "You feeling neglected? Hungry? I should see to that while you speak to her again."

Persephone nodded. "Still sure you can't be there for it?"

"This will be difficult enough without me going into a flashback of my own, trust me."

"Mandy? I have a few more questions for you."

The young woman pulled her sweater closer around her despite the heat, frowning through the screen door. It looked like she'd been crying again, and Persephone wouldn't be surprised if those were the same clothes that the girl had worn the last time she'd spoken to her. "You were just here. I thought you asked them all the last time. You asked some weird ones, too."

Persephone blamed the "weird" ones on Randolph, but she wasn't really going into that right now. She gave the younger woman a sympathetic smile, hating what she had to do, but there was no other choice. This had to be done. "I have a few more. Can I come inside?"

Mandy Berkeley moved away from the door, and Persephone took that as an invitation inside. She followed Mandy over to the couch they'd used for the last interview, and the girl sat down, making herself as small as she could on the chair. "They said there's a press conference later. Shouldn't you be there for that?"

Persephone shook her head. "Detective Batscher is going to be there. I need to be here."

"Holding my hand? Because I would much rather you just found this guy before he comes back for me," Mandy muttered. She reached for a blanket and pulled it over her. "Is it true there's a panther? Everyone's saying there's a big panther running around."

"It's a leopard, actually, but there is one. It belongs to the profiler."

Mandy stared at her. "You didn't say anything about a profiler or a leopard last time."

Persephone forced a smile. "I was trying to keep that a bit... quiet. I didn't want everyone knowing that the profiler had been brought in, and I didn't think people would understand the leopard's presence.

The profiler has been very helpful so far."

Mandy shrugged. She hadn't seen Randolph—and wouldn't—so she wouldn't know what to think about that. "I guess it would be kind of cool if the creep got bit by a leopard, huh? Or shot. Mauled to death by a leopard is better. More painful. Nothing less than he deserves."

Persephone almost laughed. She liked the idea of feeding all kinds of criminals to the leopard, but then she felt sorry about what Katya would have to eat. She almost wished the cat were here, though. Katya might do wonders for Mandy, help her feel calm and possibly even safe. Randolph couldn't do these interviews, though, and Katya was not going to leave him after Marciano showed up. "I think if we did, people would commit less crimes. They wouldn't want to face a leopard."

Mandy jumped at the knock on the door, and Persephone rose. "I'll get it."

The girl nodded, and Persephone wondered where her parents were this time. The last few times she'd tried to talk to Mandy, the Berkeleys had interrupted, trying to protect her, and while Persephone didn't like what she had to ask, blocking her wasn't helping, either. It was surprising that they'd left Mandy alone today. Persephone opened the door and looked down with a frown.

Katya pushed the screen door open and slipped in past her. Persephone frowned, looking out at Randolph, who shrugged but made no move toward the house. He leaned against his car, and Persephone shook her head as she turned back to see how much damage the cat had done.

"Wow. There really is a leopard," Mandy said, reaching a tentative hand out to pet Katya, who started purring. The girl smiled at the cat. "I think she likes me."

"She's a smart leopard," Persephone agreed, moving over to the other chair. "Mandy, I need to ask you about that morning."

"But we've done this so many times—"

"Do you always eat breakfast under that tree, sitting on your car?"

Mandy flinched, burying her face in the leopard's fur. "I didn't flirt with him."

"I know you didn't," Persephone told her, trying to keep her voice gentle, "but you *did* talk to him, didn't you?"

"I... I was just sitting there, and he called out 'nice morning, isn't it?' And I nodded, but I'd finished my sandwich. I started to clean up and was getting back in my car when... I didn't—It was just a couple words. I was being polite."

"Did you see him at all?"

"A baseball hat and some kind of... shiny jacket. Like a letter one, but... not leather. Polyester, maybe? He was just a guy, and I didn't know..." Mandy started sobbing again, and Persephone sighed. Katya licked the girl's face, and she held tight onto the leopard.

After a few minutes, Mandy lifted her head again. "Um... I can't think of—it was the style. No letter on it, but so like that type. Not from the school here, though. It had gold sleeves and was black or blue or red... I don't know. It was—I didn't see his face. Didn't see anything. He didn't even... scare me. I was just packing up because I was done."

"Did you notice any kind of accent when he spoke?"

"No. None. He could have been local," Mandy looked down at the leopard. "Is... is it my fault, what happened to the other girls? Because I didn't tell you about that? I should have..."

She started crying again, and Persephone was glad the leopard was there because she had no idea what she would have said. It wasn't like she wanted to blame the girl, but there had been victims after Mandy, and what she'd admitted this morning could have stopped something—or not. It was hard to say, but the last thing Mandy needed was more guilt. "What I am going to do now is take what you've told me and put it together with everything else we have and hope that we keep getting enough of these little pieces to find this man. Katya is going to sit with you while I go outside for a minute."

"Okay."

"Your leopard is taking over my case."

"She does that."

"I thought you were taking her to feed her."

Randolph shrugged, going over to Reynolds' car. She followed him, taking out the hat and sunglasses she'd left behind when she walked up to do her interview. After putting them back on, she started reapplying the sunscreen. He didn't know why she was so resistant to the hat. It suited her. "When the leopard hisses and growls and threatens to dismantle the car, I pull over. I thought it was you she sought, honestly."

"She knew that Mandy needed her," Reynolds admitted, looking back at the house and letting out a breath. She closed her eyes and shook her head. "Now that girl wants to blame herself for not telling us, and I don't know—I didn't have any idea what to say to her. Would it really help if she knew that it has almost nothing to do with her and is really about this other woman that she vaguely resembles? Probably not. And what she gave us isn't groundbreaking—Bite Boy told us about the baseball hat and jacket, and even if we put that out there, how many women would it have helped? I don't honestly believe that he always wears that hat and jacket—no one else mentioned gold sleeves or shiny material, either."

Randolph had been about to reach out and comfort her when his latest thought derailed him, taking his mind in a different direction. "A letter jacket?"

Reynolds nodded. "You're taking this back to the college thing, aren't you? She said it wasn't local."

"We're still talking about a recreation. He might have *dozens* of those jackets, different colors and schools—if they even have schools on them. It's not about the school—it's the time and the feeling that it represents."

"He was standing in the letter jacket when she rejected him? Doesn't that make this more... high school, then? That's the wrong age for the victims, though."

"Not necessarily," Randolph disagreed. "Not if he was *younger* than the woman in question."

"The letter jacket made him feel like a man, and she laughed and ruined that for him?"

Randolph frowned. His mind was torn in too many directions, and it was hard to focus on one thing in particular. His half-formed theory with the letter jacket had now morphed, and he didn't like the latest direction his thoughts had taken.

Reynolds put a hand on his arm. "I'm going to go check on Mandy and see if I can convince her to call someone to stay with her for a while. Try not to hurt yourself with all that thinking you're doing."

"Reynolds, did you have any male friends in high school?"

"Excuse me? What does that have to do with anything?"

"Any of them with a crush on your older sister?"

"No. And if I did, as much as it would bother me, I'd tell you," Reynolds assured him. Randolph frowned again. "I mean it. I didn't— Angie was my best friend in high school, and while she had her fair share of guys hanging around, I never did."

"Why not? You're a very beautiful woman."

Her cheeks took on a slight pink tinge, not all that noticeable a shade despite her claims that she'd turn into a red queen with the sunburn she had yet to acquire. "If you must know, when Jake Moore tried to kiss me in ninth grade, he was so clumsy that he missed my mouth. I smacked him for licking my ear, and thus cemented my reputation as an unreachable ice queen. It wasn't even so much what I did as the rumors that went around afterward. He made up all kinds of... cruel, hateful things to go along with the idea of me being 'Frosty,' and most of the guys were too afraid of losing their equipment to risk dating me."

"You're not frosty."

She rolled her eyes. Randolph shrugged. "I would know, wouldn't I?"

"That—that was just one kiss for the press, and I have to go check on Mandy."

Chapter Eight

She wasn't avoiding him.

She *wanted* to, but they had work to do. She couldn't afford to act like a teenager—a child—and get weird about the conversation they'd had or the observations he'd made. It was one thing when he picked up on things from her past, when he poked at the old wounds surrounding her father's death. That made her defensive, angry, and she retaliated.

This was different. This knocked her for a different type of loop, and she was used to the anger, could channel it and the pain into something that helped her get more work done. This made her skin crawl, made her aware of every time his eyes fell on her, and she would almost rather he saw her as a psychological problem to unravel than a woman. She never should have kissed him. It was a moment she wished she could take back. She'd done it without giving enough thought to the consequences—oh, she'd thought of her mother and the jokes that would go around the department but not that it could make things awkward between the two of them. It hadn't, surprisingly enough. He'd gone right to work at that dump site, and they'd progressed from there without mentioning what had happened.

Why had he brought that up now, of all times? They were discussing what Mandy told them, not... them. There was no *them*. That was—It was a part of his theory about Persephone's sister, a theory that he couldn't seem to let go.

"Any connections?" Persephone asked, looking over at Randolph as he finished his phone call.

"No. Mrs. Marcie didn't find anything."

"Mrs. Marcie?"

Randolph shrugged. "I do it out of affection, really. He hates it— being called 'Marcie,' I mean—and extending the nickname to her was a way of... welcoming her to the family, as it were."

"Right."

He smiled at her for a moment. "How is the girl?"

"Sleeping. The leopard's good at that, too."

"Doesn't quite work on you, but yes," Randolph agreed. He put his phone back on his belt and sighed. "I feel as though something is missing."

"This guy's arrest, you mean?"

Randolph gave her another slight smile, and Persephone wondered, just for a moment, if getting their chemistry out of the way was the best way to handle it—but no, he was just here for this case, and when he was gone, that would be gone with him, and things would go back to the way they always were. Persephone was fine with that. Besides, the case was far more important than any physical attraction they might have.

"An arrest is still possible, but we need the missing pieces first," Randolph began, rubbing his forehead. He leaned back against the car. "It's frustrating. I—I have so many small parts, little bits of the puzzle, and I am pulled in so many directions that I'm not getting anywhere with my thoughts. I'm just jumbling things about, giving myself another headache."

"Maybe you need some time to let yourself process them. Something to take your mind off of it for long enough for one part to clarify a little."

"Perhaps."

"Maybe you need to let the leopard put you to bed this time."

He laughed. "I have to admit—I keep thinking I should run while I have the chance. Still, she'll find me, and I don't... I don't *hate* her. It's just difficult to find a chance to breathe with a leopard stalking me. Sometimes her presence is a true comfort, others... it is suffocating. It is hard to balance these things."

Persephone nodded. "Still, if you were going to take the time to sleep, this would be it. We've got nothing from your theory, still no id on the girl he killed, no real way to make the list of registered gun owners smaller—and no right to go harass them just for owning one—"

"Second amendment rights. Yes. Though for elimination's sake, we could ask all of them to let us check their weapons to see if they've been fired recently and for a possible match to the bullet we recovered. It would be strictly voluntary and infringe on no one's rights."

"Yes, and that's really the only way to handle it at this point. I still don't think the registration is going to give us the answer we want."

"He would be foolish to use a weapon that can trace back to him, but if we did not check that list, we would not be doing our jobs."

"Which is why BB assigned a few uniforms to start that canvas after he got our list. I just wanted the list narrowed down further," Persephone agreed. "The bases are covered, aren't they? You can take time for yourself now, get some sleep. Hell, I'll take a few hours if that's what you're worried about."

"It isn't. No, we should return to the station. There's something..."

"What?"

He winced. "I don't know. I can't quit until I figure out what it is, but it's nagging at me. Has been all day despite everything, and I know I have to settle it before I have any hope of resting. We can check on those covered bases and possibly take a section of the list for ourselves, but I cannot stop now."

"Randolph—"

"Don't. Don't say I can stop. I walked away once and because I did, because I didn't stay where that man thought I should be, he took another woman, and he killed her. I can't stop when I feel like this no matter how tired I am or how much my head aches. This is the part I can't forgive myself for."

Persephone shook her head. "None of it is your fault."

"Like you don't believe this is somehow your failure as well," Randolph scoffed. He shook his head. "If I can at least pin down what's bothering me now—something about the jacket, perhaps, or something more—I am not certain—then I agree we should both try and take some time to sleep because we both need it. I just need this first."

Persephone added letter jacket to the list on her board and stepped back with a frown. The leopard bumped her leg, and she reached down to pet her as she studied the board. The list was short, too short. It wasn't enough. Not nearly enough. "I don't like this."

"Can't say I blame you," Marciano agreed. "Randolph? You still with us over there?"

"Another headache?" Persephone asked, turning back from the board. He shook his head, and Marciano gave him a pointed look. The leopard growled, but not at Marciano. She was still staring at the board. "What?"

"He's going to kill again. Tonight. If she isn't already dead."

Persephone winced. "How—No, I don't want to know. You're sure about this?"

"Instinct, possibly my own experience talking. I don't... It's been bothering me for a while, but I got caught up in other facets of this case and ignored it. No, I think he's already taken someone else," Randolph said, getting to his feet. Katya moved over to his side, and he looked down at her. "I know. We'll find him, and you can bite him. Sound good to you, love? Yes, I thought you'd like that."

"If you're right, we know the kind of areas this guy uses as dump sites," Marciano reminded them. "We take the time now, grid the areas, make sure the uniforms know to keep an eye on these alleyways, maybe we can catch him in the act. Well, not exactly, but you know what I mean."

Persephone nodded. They'd already told the patrol cars to be on the lookout for that, and she'd been fighting to get some of the traffic ones rerouted to keep an eye on possible dump sites for a while now. Maybe if Randolph and Marciano added their opinions to that and Marciano's federal authority—as unofficial as it was—into that suggestion, someone would listen this time.

Only if they saw this, they might not think much of the profiler's expertise, not right now. He'd dropped to the floor, curled up into a ball, whispering to himself. He didn't seem to notice Katya's attempts to get him to look at her. "Randolph?"

"Oh, damn it, that's a flashback," Marciano said. He shook his head. "I'm not sure which of us would be better—if we can get through to him at all. He might hear the woman if you try to reach him, and if I do, the killer. Come on, cat. Growl and remind him you're here."

Katya bumped her head against Randolph's chest, and he jerked. "Let her go. Don't do this. Don't."

Persephone knelt next to them. "Randolph, she's free. Nothing is going to happen to her, not anymore."

"Please," he begged, still not back with them despite the leopard licking his face. He shuddered and pulled away from Katya, smacking into the desk.

Persephone looked up at Marciano. "Any ideas?"

"I don't know. He hasn't been like this in a long time, and back then, we just rode it out. Well, it'll probably trigger a headache soon enough, and he'll pass out because of the pain. He told me he hadn't had any since the leopard came along."

"Well, that's great, but clearly this case threw that out the window," Persephone said, almost snapping the words. She took hold of Randolph's hand. "Do we—Can we move him? If anyone else comes through here, they won't understand. BB already expressed plenty of doubts that Randolph could help us with this case, and with the leopard and the stunt I pulled in front of the press, Randolph could lose all credibility here. We know he needs that."

"Yeah," Marciano said, moving closer. "Come on, Katya, out of the way."

Persephone felt pressure on her hand and looked down at it before she caught Randolph's eyes on her. He took a deep breath. "I... I lost it for a minute, didn't I?"

"Yeah, you did," Marciano agreed. "Think you can get up, *amico?*"

"Not really, but I have to," Randolph muttered, dragging himself up with their help. "I don't... How bad was I?"

"No screaming. You did beg a couple times."

"Need to get out of here," Randolph said, moving toward the door. "Can't believe I did that."

"You kidding? I'm surprised it didn't happen sooner."

"Go to hell, Marcie."

"You look... bad."

Randolph didn't want to look at her. She was right, but he didn't feel like agreeing with her, and he was still having trouble making the images and voices fade. Marcie had offered to drive, giving the leopard the front seat and letting Reynolds sit in back with Randolph. Marcie seemed to feel that it was her act of holding his hand and not any action on part of the leopard that had drawn Randolph out of that hell, and while Randolph did not want to agree, he had been more revolted by Katya's help than aided. He had never liked it when his pets licked him, even as fond as he had been of the puppy he'd had in his youth.

"Are you going to try and pull me off this case now?"

"No, but I am forcing you to take the rest of the night off," Reynolds told him. This time he did look over at her. She shook her head. "You're not arguing with me. You won't win. You were tired before, but after that... Besides, you told me you'd be willing to rest if you figured out what was bothering you, and you did."

"Reynolds—"

"You can't do anything until the body shows up anyway."

He winced, shaking his head and shuddering at the images that flashed before his eyes. He was nauseous, ready to lose what little he'd eaten earlier. The shovel, the screams... He forced them out of his mind. "And you?"

"I'm going to coordinate our efforts to catch this bastard when he comes out tonight."

Randolph put a hand to his head. He was still struggling to organize what he was thinking. He knew there was so much there. He needed to sort it out, but that old case was getting in the way again. He shuddered, hating his own reaction to all of this.

She touched his hand, and his eyes flew to hers. "You need to take this time."

"I... I don't like this. I know I just had a panic attack and a flashback, and I can't blame you for questioning my judgment, but something is... wrong. It's off. It's bad. It's... I hate this helplessness. Not being able to do anything until he acts, knowing even if we beg, we can't stop him..."

"You tried to get him to stop the only way you could."

"Asking. Yeah. Right. That does not work. Not with people like them."

"That is why we do what we do. The little pieces will add up eventually, Randolph. It won't be easy, and it's not going to be short, but we know we'll get him as long as we keep working at it. Even if it's through some random theory of yours. I don't care how we find him as long as we do, and I know you can still contribute to this, but you have to let this take its course. You have to let yourself recover first."

He let out a breath. If he was honest about it, he didn't want to be left alone with his memories, but he would not be. He had the leopard. "I doubt I will get much of any rest, and I would much rather be working."

"Yeah. I know how that goes, but you're outvoted here. As soon as we get to my mother's house, I'm going to have the leopard keep you there. And don't think she won't. She's that protective of you," Reynolds said, and Katya started to purr, voicing her rather loud agreement.

"Yeah, I know she is."

"She's not the only one," Marcie commented. "Hell, I'd make you stay myself, but the leopard's better at it than me."

"You're going with Reynolds, though. She needs as much help as she can get trying to catch this guy tonight. It'll be an alley. I keep going back and forth over whether or not he'd use one he did before. Maybe. He has to know we'd watch them, though. I don't know. It might not be important to him. Or it could be everything. I can't... It's not clear."

"Stop trying to break your brain," Reynolds teased, patting his hand again. "We'll watch the old sites and try and cover as many of the new ones as we can. That's the best we can do. You are going to rest. And between the leopard and my mother—"

"That is almost vindictive of you, Reynolds."

She shook her head. "No. She'll take good care of you. They both will."

Persephone hated waiting.

She wasn't sure she knew anyone that liked it, honestly. She knew people that made it a game—Angie liked to make up stories about the people she saw passing by, and she could see Randolph doing something similar, being a profiler like he was—but Persephone wasn't one of those people, and even if she was, she couldn't afford to make this into a game. Not unless she wanted to miss something.

She gave the radio a dirty look as she heard another round of bitching from one of the surveillance teams. They didn't think much of their assignment, and she knew that Randolph's hunch wasn't much to go on, not for most of them, but the way his conviction had taken him down plus the other insights he'd had into this bastard were enough for her.

That was a switch. She tended to be of the opinion that shrinks were just pushy know-it-alls that didn't have any business evaluating her or her colleagues, no right to tell them what they were doing was wrong. She shook her head. Randolph wasn't one of them. Though he'd pushed way too far into her private life with all the questions he asked about her father and sister, Persephone had to admire the way he fought to be a part of this case despite what it was doing to him.

He had better be sleeping. He needed to get some rest, and he deserved having her mother fussing over him. Besides, this way she wouldn't be worrying about what Persephone was doing right now. Not that Persephone was doing anything at the moment.

She sighed. The idiots on the radio might be right about this. It might be a complete waste of time, an overreaction. It might give them nothing. She didn't want to think about that. She wanted to believe that they were going to get this bastard. She wanted to get to him *tonight.*

She slowed her car down as she drove past the alley again. She'd been by this one a few times already, her own circuit, a bigger part of the grid than she'd hoped for, but without more than Randolph's gut to go on—even with Marciano's backing—they hadn't gotten as many people assigned to this as she'd hoped for, and though they'd pulled in a few units from the county sheriff's office and highway patrol, it wasn't enough.

Something moved in the alley, and she stopped her car. It might be nothing, but she had to check it out anyway. She picked up her radio. "This is Reynolds. May have something behind the grocery off ninth."

"It'll be a cat. Oh, wait, you left the leopard at home," a smart aleck teased through the radio, and she rolled her eyes as she clipped the handset to her belt and took out her gun.

She walked down the alley, keeping her steps slow and careful, listening for any sign of someone's presence. It could have been an animal, could have been another homeless man, or it could have been nothing. She could be jumping at shadows here.

"Damn," she said after she passed the dumpster. Randolph had been right, again. Persephone looked down at the woman. "I'm sorry."

She looked around her. She didn't see any other way out, but her stomach twisted. She couldn't help feeling uneasy. Had she seen nothing, then? Just... instinct calling her back to where he'd slipped by her when she drove past a different alley? Or was he here?

She didn't see anything. She let out a breath and took out her radio as she returned to the body. "Yeah, I got something. A body. I need a crime scene unit and—"

Something grabbed hold of her and yanked her backward, slamming her head against the building. She lost the radio but tightened her hold on the gun as the baseball cap tried to knock it out of her hand, keeping it angled away from him so that she couldn't get a good shot, his other arm up against her neck, cutting off her air supply. She struggled, kicking at his leg only to have him smack her head into the brick again. She pulled the trigger, hoping the gun shot would work in place of a scream as the combination of what he'd done to her forced her to lose consciousness.

Chapter Nine

"Are you sure you don't need anything else?"

"No, Lillian, thank you," Randolph said, thinking he already had far too much food in front of him and not nearly enough appetite to deal with it. "If you wish, perhaps you should see if Katya needs more. Or perhaps she should come back inside. I know that the dark might have helped with your neighbors tonight, but I do not know that you should continue to encourage her to eat outside."

"I do appreciate you cleaning my floor after the first time she was here, but I much prefer her eating outside," Lillian told him, taking his water glass and going to refill it. He sighed, shaking his head a little. Despite what Reynolds had said, this did seem to be more like a punishment. Lillian was more than attentive.

Of course, Reynolds would *not* be pleased to hear that he'd asked as many questions about her sister as he had. He could tell that Lillian found it odd. She kept trying to sneak in some mention of her other daughter, misunderstanding his purpose. He was not interested in Sarah Reynolds in any romantic sense, and his admiration for Persephone remained untainted by what he learned of the one they called Sunny. What he needed, though, was a way to prove or disprove the theory that had come to him when he first saw that family picture.

He rose and returned to it, studying it again. Sarah looked almost the same as her mother, and with them both, the smiles were easy and natural. The young man was relaxed, a near exact replica of his father—perhaps the reason for his current distance was that resemblance. One that strong could cause a great degree of pain to his family as much as they missed having him nearby—and both men seemed comfortable. The one that didn't was the one that, at first glance, did not belong at all. On closer examination, she had the features of each of her parents—the eyes from her mother, her father's nose—though that did little to change the discomfort she felt when compared to her family.

The realization he had then shook him again, and he told himself he had to be wrong. It was just the flashback unsettling him, nothing more.

"Randolph?"

He looked over at Mrs. Reynolds. She gave him a very uncomfortable smile. He frowned. "Was I... Did I... 'zone out' again?"

"Um... A bit, yes, but... Actually, I don't quite know how to tell you this, but your leopard..." Lillian took a deep breath. "Your leopard seems to be missing."

"Missing?"

"I doubt that the humane society could have come for her even if my neighbors complained—"

Randolph dug out his phone and moved away from her, going to the other room as he made the call. "Marcie, where's Reynolds?"

"I am not sure I want to know how you knew to call. She just radioed in that she might have something—"

"Where is she? I need to know *now,*" Randolph interrupted, picking up Mrs. Reynolds' keys off the counter in the kitchen.

"Randolph—"

"Katya's gone. Tell me where Reynolds is *now,*" Randolph ordered, moving toward the door. He saw the worried look on the older Reynolds' face and winced. She should not have heard that.

"Grocery store off ninth," Marciano said, and Randolph hung up.

He turned to Reynolds' mother. "They found something. I need to borrow your car."

"It's your leopard, right?"

Randolph nodded. He looked past the uniform that asked, drawing close to the cat pacing in agitation, baring her teeth, growling and snapping at anyone who tried to approach. He gave her a look, shaking his head. "Katya, you have to let them look at her."

The leopard blinked. He knelt next to her. "I know you claimed the detective, but if she's hurt, she needs to see a doctor. You have to let us look at her."

Katya moved, letting Randolph past and taking up a sentry position behind him. He shifted closer to Reynolds, studying her with care, trying to find every wound. He could see blood staining some of the strands of her hair, and he tried to control his reaction to that, though it was not easy. He reached over to brush back the part that had fallen on her neck, thinking he saw a mark there, a discoloration of some kind.

"Swore... nothing... there..."

"Good to see you're still with us, Persephone. One might have thought you were taking up the role from your myth," Randolph said, giving her a slight smile. "No, no, don't move, not until we get those EMTs over to get a good look at you."

"Just... hat... Only saw... hat..."

"Rest," he told her, applying a gentle pressure to her shoulder to keep her from moving. She shouldn't get up. They didn't know how badly hurt she was yet. "I know you want to keep working through this, but you can't. Not now."

She closed her eyes again. "Couldn't... breathe..."

"You're talking to a man who got whacked over the head with a shovel and never saw it coming. You don't have to defend yourself to me."

"Almost... one... Think... car... cat... Can't... remember..."

Randolph was already painfully aware that she could have been this man's next victim. Unplanned, yes, because she'd interrupted him as he dumped the body. It bothered Randolph that he'd confronted her instead of waiting for her to leave. If Randolph understood her correctly, their suspect had been in the process of dragging her off when Katya intervened.

"More of it might come back later—or not at all," Randolph told Reynolds, taking her hand and frowning again at the sight of her wrist.

"Cat... saved... my life..."

He shrugged. "She likes you."

"How?"

"Plenty to like about you." Randolph got bumped, and he looked at Katya with a frown. The cat fell against him, and he shook his head, not sure how to cope with the fact that he'd very nearly lost both of them. "Marcie!"

The FBI agent pushed his way past the others in the crowd. "Let the EMTs take her—"

"Need a vet, too, damn it."

"Oh, hell."

"If you hold her still, I'll take a look."

Randolph nodded, numb, looking down at Katya. Her head was in his lap, her eyes closed, and he was running his fingers through her fur as he watched her side rise and fall. She was still breathing. He had to hold onto that. Not literally, of course. His other hand was still holding onto Reynolds even though she had fallen unconscious again. The other EMT was still assessing her, but the man closest to him had volunteered to look at the leopard.

"Kitty's a hero, huh?"

"Heroine," Randolph corrected, watching the man comb through the fur on the leopard's side. The EMT let out a whistle and above him, Marciano cursed. "How bad?"

"It's a graze, but it cut her pretty deep along the way."

"Guy took Reynolds' gun," Marcie added after the EMT finished speaking. "Probably shot at Katya when she tried to stop him. Well, no, she didn't just try. She definitely stopped him from doing anything else to Reynolds. And that's not her blood on her claws, either."

Randolph gave the leopard a grim smile. "Good girl, Katya. Very, very good girl."

"Sir? We need to move now," the other EMT interrupted, looking at the hand that still held Persephone's. "We'll check her out at the hospital, but it looks like a concussion. She got knocked around a bit, but she should be fine."

"Randolph, you want me to take Katya to the vet while you go with Reynolds?"

Katya opened her eyes when Marciano said that, letting out a growl as the EMTs started to lift Reynolds onto their stretcher. Randolph tried to calm her down again. "They need to take her to the hospital, love. And you need care, too."

The leopard ignored him, running over and jumping into the back of the ambulance. She laid down again, closing her eyes. Marciano sighed. "This seems rather familiar."

"Yes," Randolph agreed, getting to his feet and going over to the ambulance. "Katya, this is not the same as claiming me. You can't stay with Reynolds right now. You have to let us take you to a vet. You're hurt."

She gave him a growl, and Marciano shook his head. *"Amico,* if she's snapping at *you,* of all people, there is no way that you're going to get her away from Reynolds."

The EMTs gave him a look, hesitating when they should be loading Reynolds into the ambulance. Randolph shrugged, feeling helpless. "I'll ride with them and keep her calm. She won't do anything to you, but I don't think you—or anyone—can separate her from Reynolds at the moment. Katya doesn't back off when she's assumed protection of someone, trust me on that. Marciano, you will call Mrs. Reynolds and let her know to meet us at the hospital?"

"Yeah, just as soon as I make sure they know you're coming in

138

with a leopard," Marcie agreed. He waved Randolph on. "Get in there. Take care of them. I'll hold down the fort here for a bit longer and meet you there."

"Marcie—"

"No. You know you need me. And for the last time, lay off the damn 'Marcie' crap."

"Thank you, Marcie," Randolph said, using the name on purpose, climbing into the back of the ambulance. He took hold of Reynolds' hand again, reaching for the leopard with his other hand, not sure how much longer he'd be able to hold it together. Reynolds should never have been alone in that alley, and Katya... He didn't know how the leopard had known, but somehow she always did.

He looked over when he felt Reynolds squeeze his hand, and her eyes met his. "Tell me... I didn't shoot the leopard."

"What?"

"Couldn't scream. Couldn't shoot him. Did fire the gun."

Randolph shook his head. "I don't—I got there after it was all over. I don't know. She was grazed. She'll be fine, and she won't leave you which I don't think would be the case if you had shot her..."

Reynolds nodded and then grimaced. "Head... hurts..."

"You have a concussion at the very least."

"Don't call... No... No late night call for my mother. Please."

"You can't not tell her."

"Not another phone call. Not like my dad."

Randolph winced. "Marcie was going to talk to her. I'm sorry. I didn't think of that before, didn't tell him to go in person. I should have thought of that. I didn't."

Katya licked his fingers, and he sighed. "Yes, Katya, I know I was distracted. It's no excuse."

"Don't... start blaming yourself for this, Randolph."

He looked at Reynolds. It was already too late for that.

"How is the fort?"

"Rattled. Lot of them thought this was a waste of time, but not only did the guy leave another body, he got close to one of their own. That ice queen myth has already gone a bit too far—I don't think they thought anything could happen to her—but she's here," Marciano explained, looking over at the detective and then to the cot beside her. "I see the leopard got the proper special treatment."

Randolph rose from the chair next to the bed and studied the figure on the small cot they'd brought in, a concession made out of fear after numerous arguments about hospital policy. "She was not very cooperative, not even after her arrival here, and she did not want them taking Reynolds for the appropriate scans. I believe that the staff feels much better now that Katya has been suitably treated—and by that I mean drugged—and is resting to tend to her own injuries. Though there were several comments about how the dosage must have been wrong when she continued her push to see Reynolds."

"That's tame. I know because I saw what she was like trying to get to you—and that was after you rescued *her*, not the other way around," Marciano observed, crossing over to give the sleeping leopard a pet. Katya's eyes opened for a moment, but she didn't lift her head from the cot. "She's still a fighter."

"I know." The leopard was far stronger than she looked—and that said something because she was a rather intimidating animal to begin with. Randolph had seen her ignore far worse injuries and pain to get to what she wanted, and so had Marcie.

"Had to send a uni over to pick up Reynolds' mother since you had her car and left it at the scene," Marciano went on, his eyes going to the woman this time. "How is she?"

"Concussion, few bruises, no major damage. Could have been a lot worse—he very nearly strangled her—was doing his best to crush her windpipe—as he dragged her out of that alley, and if he had taken her..."

"Randolph, you know this isn't your fault."

"Don't start with me, Marcie, I'm not in the mood," Randolph warned, looking away, past the other man and to the doorway. "Is her mother here, then?"

"No. You are not doing what you think you're doing."

Randolph gave the other man a dark look. "You have no idea what is going through my head at the moment, and do not even pretend to guess."

"Yeah, sure I don't. I haven't been your friend long enough to know that you somehow believe this is all your fault. That Reynolds got hurt because of you. That the leopard did, too. That your flashback earlier let everyone down, that you should be better than that, over all that crap in the past, and should have been there with her. You know better than anyone that this kind of thing can happen to anyone. Even if she hadn't been alone, that guy could have gotten to her. Hell, you were in the middle of the biggest crime scene in the city when you got hit with a shovel and taken out right under all of our noses. You think that sits well with me? Seems to me, though, you told me several times that wasn't my fault. You meant it was yours, but if I'm not to blame there, you're not to blame, either. Not then and not now."

"The face... the voice... they've blurred. It's her now, Marcie. I can't do this. I *can't.*"

"*Maledizione,*" Marciano whispered. "Randolph—"

"I spent the evening asking about my crackpot theory while he was... while she... I don't—I thought I could do this, but I can't. The lines are blurred, the memories... I can't do this. I can't... My judgment

142

is compromised. That's not something you can ignore."

"Randolph—"

"I'm done, Marcie. Accept that."

Chapter Ten

Persephone's head ached like she'd been on the kind of binge she hadn't known since her brother graduated college, and she lifted her hand to touch the back of her head. Her fingers touched gauze, and she frowned. No, she did remember—he'd put her head into the back of a brick building *twice*—and she found swallowing very difficult. It all hurt. That was an exaggeration, but that was how it felt at first. She opened her eyes and looked right at a leopard.

"I'd say I was on drugs, but I know that cat."

"You're still on drugs, sweetie, but that doesn't mean you don't know the cat," her mother said, smiling at her as she took her hand. Persephone looked over at her. She'd never wanted to do this to her mother, not again. The hospital wasn't the morgue, but it was too damn close.

"Why am I seeing the cat and not its owner?"

Lillian laughed. "That's a joke. That cat isn't owned by anyone. That cat owns the man—and now it would seem like she owns you, too."

Persephone sighed. "That is not what I meant. I don't care about ownership. I need to get out of this bed and get back to work. Where is

Randolph?"

"You're not going anywhere, Persephone. They want to keep an eye on you for a bit longer. The concussion was grade three, whatever that means, and you've been in and out all night. All day. You're staying where you are, and you're going to get better. There are other cops that can handle this case while you recover. You have to give this a bit of time."

"I know you're worried about me, Mom, but I am not sitting in this bed a minute longer than I have to, and that means that now that I'm awake, I'm done. I am not lying around in bed, not now," Persephone insisted, pulling out her IV. She didn't need it. She was sore, but she was fine. What mattered to her now was getting the bastard that had done this to her before he hurt anyone else.

"Persephone!" Lillian cried, trying to force her back down on the bed. Her head spun, and her mother won for the moment. "Stay put. Leopard, you make her do it. You did it to him; you can do it to her. She's not allowed to move."

"Where are they? Marciano and Randolph?"

"Marciano is back at the station. I hope you're not going to get mad at him. I think they're about to hand this thing over to him, and I, for my part, like the idea, especially after this."

"Mom, I'm fine," Persephone repeated. She started to sit up again, and this time the leopard growled. She looked over at Katya, reaching to touch her head. "That goes for you, too, Katya. I'm fine. Now where is your profiler, hmm?"

Katya lowered her head, staring at Persephone for a long moment. She had never in her life seen a cat look that mournful. "If you're begging, I don't have anything for you. I'm sure you're hungry, though. Why haven't you made Randolph take you for food? I'm sure they can't keep you here."

Katya jumped up on the bed. Persephone winced when she saw the bandages wrapped around the cat's stomach. "Oh, Katya."

The leopard purred, snuggling up close to her. Persephone combed through the cat's fur, sighing. "Okay, I don't get it. Why are you here and not him?"

Katya closed her eyes, no longer purring. Persephone shook her head and closed her eyes again. She didn't understand why the leopard had stayed with her. Sure, she was hurt, but not that badly. She wasn't the one that Katya had bonded with. "You know how to find him, don't you?"

The leopard put a paw on Persephone's arm. She took that as a yes. She would get up in a little while, when her head stopped hurting.

"Didn't figure you'd be out of bed yet, Reynolds."

"They didn't want to let me out," she agreed, grateful for the hat that covered the bandage on her head. It was there to cover the stitches, but she knew it was like a beacon, and she'd have to go into a stylist sometime and even out what they'd done to her hair when they put in the stitches. "I wasn't about to stay, though. We have too much to do."

BB shook his head. "We can get a formal statement from you later. Go home."

"Not going to happen," she muttered, reaching down to touch Katya's head. "Marciano around?"

"Big wig's in with the other big wigs. You're a mess. Go home."

"Like hell, BB. I was standing in that alley, I swore I checked it, and he still got the better of me. Not going home. Not stopping until I get this bastard. He's going to pay for what he did to my head and that cat, are we clear?" Persephone demanded. "Good. Now tell me what we've got."

"Maybe a break. At least with the press. Check out the cover story."

"'Heroic Leopard Saves Local Cop,'" she read off, shaking her head again. She skimmed the article with a frown. "There's nothing here about the second body, nothing here about why I was in that alley. They barely even mentioned the fact that I'm working on the serial rapist case that they've been following and hounding me about

147

for the past six weeks. Half the article is on what makes a leopard melanistic, and the other is a sensationalized report of what happened that doesn't—it's *not* what happened. He bashed my head against the building, and he cut off my air so I couldn't breathe, couldn't fight back, but he did *not* do that."

"Everyone who needs to know knows what really happened."

"Yeah, but the other women he attacked have one thing I do not—anonymity," Persephone snapped, wadding up the paper and throwing it in the garbage. "Let's talk about the woman I found. Do we have an id for her? I didn't get much of a chance to look before he smacked me into the building."

"Here," Marciano said, walking up to them. "Take the file with you. Make sure he gets a good look at it."

Persephone looked at him. "Randolph hasn't seen this?"

Marciano shook his head. "The leopard wasn't the only thing he left behind."

She nodded, rubbing her head. Katya gave a low growl, and Persephone looked down at the leopard. "I thought you were going to find him. That was the plan, wasn't it, kitty?"

BB frowned. "What are we discussing now? I thought we—What happened to you, anyway? You cross over, Reynolds? The feds going to offer you a big time job after all this is done?"

"More like a ring," Marciano muttered, and Persephone shot him a look. "Circus one, right? Since you've inherited the leopard."

"Inherited? That's gonna be permanent? Thought the leopard came with the profiler—and I haven't seen the profiler since he went to the hospital with you," BB added. He rubbed his forehead. "You know what, I don't need to know. One good thing did come of the fed connection, though. We finally got an id on our first dead girl."

"Passing motorist?" Persephone asked, and Marciano nodded. "It was one of his off-hand suggestions, but he was right. Again."

"Randolph is good at what he does. One of the best, actually."

"The family got notified?"

"They will be. I'll have a local agent go out and do it in person. We've only confirmed the car, not the girl. They'll want to claim the body, but it won't happen right away. There's nothing here but a bunch of politics, and none of them will want you back here yet. You may as well take the day."

"I just got done telling BB—"

"Give us a minute, Batscher," Marciano ordered, and BB hesitated, but only for a moment, and then he walked away. Marciano looked at her. "Look, you know as well as I do that Randolph's head is nowhere near on straight, and I didn't think I'd see the day when he walked away from the leopard."

"Still don't see how she let him go."

"In case you haven't noticed, the leopard claimed you, too.

Meaning she had to pick. You were wounded, so she stayed with you."

"I'm not—I don't understand. She's his leopard. When did I even start to factor into this?"

"Ask Katya. I don't know. I do know that you're probably the only one that's going to get him to look past that guilt. He's in it so deep that he doesn't even know where he is right now. He's got it in his head that what happened to you was his fault."

"Why? He might have called the second murder, but that doesn't mean he's the one that hit me over the head or shot the leopard. He's—"

"Tell him that. Tell him *you* don't blame him. Then you and the leopard drag him back here so that he finishes this. He needs to see this through. You know that. I know that. He can't see it right now, but he will."

Persephone sighed. She looked down. "You know where he is?"

"She will. Just get in the car, start driving. She'll tell you where to turn."

"Can I ask you a question?"

"You mean, why I would do all this for him?" Marciano asked, smiling. "Owe him. Cases, friendship, my life. Owe the leopard, too. She's... Well, Katya's got a bit of a matchmaking talent. She's the reason I'm a happily married man."

"I guess I thought I'd find you somewhere else, especially looking this contemplative."

Randolph couldn't look at her, couldn't look at the leopard as she nudged his leg and put her head under his hand. He continued to study the barren ground in front of him. The weeds had yet to overtake the lot, though in some places they had done a remarkable job. Still, he thought it best that nothing grew here, and he knew he was not the only one. "You figured on a cemetery?"

"Is that so unusual?"

"Typical, actually, and the place most people might be, but if we must touch upon the religious aspect of things... I think we should say that I do not believe there is any part of her to talk to at that grave and leave it at that."

Reynolds moved up to stand next to him, shaking her head. "I didn't really figure you for this kind of masochist, Randolph. Coming back to where you watched her die? That's more than a little... cruel, don't you think?"

"I'd see the images no matter where I was, so this is no different from anywhere else."

"I don't think so. The families of those women took this land from his family and tore the building down. They didn't want it staying up, and I can't say I blame them. He tortured their wives and daughters and sisters here. And you."

"He barely touched me, other than the shovel to the back of the head, that is."

Reynolds touched Randolph's arm. "What you *saw* was the torture, and don't try and say it wasn't. You heard and saw things no one wants to see or hear. He hurt you without touching you. It happens. 'Psychological warfare.' You know that term, don't you?"

Randolph turned to face her. As much as he liked the look of her with the hat, he had to take it off, looking at the bandage on her head with a wince. She took the hat back. "This? It was not you. It was not your fault. It was him, and the important part now is not who gets the blame. The point is finding that bastard and making him pay."

"Reynolds, I can't help you. I can't see this thing for what it is, and I am *no* use to you like this."

She shook her head. "You have been right about just about *everything* to do with this case. You pegged the first dead woman as a passing motorist, and you were right. You have seen a lot of things on this case that we missed, and you know what? We almost caught him because of your instinct that he'd killed again."

"You could have died."

"I kind of took that on when I took the badge. Sure, the last time that happened for someone around my hometown was almost twenty years ago, but that's not the point. It was a risk I always knew was a part of the job. The thing that gets me about it is that I *know* I checked that alley. I know there was no one there. And then he was. If not for your leopard..."

Randolph shook his head. "She doesn't belong with me. No one does. Take her. She likes you. She'll protect you through the end of this."

"It's not like she suddenly stopped caring about you, Randolph. She's still your leopard."

"I am not coming back with you, Reynolds. I can't hardly even *look* at you right now. I see you and not her. Hear you and not her. Go away. I can't do this. I *won't* do this. I can't help you. I can't make this stop..."

"This case is how you stop it. You fight all the way through it this time."

"No."

"Didn't figure you for a quitter."

He shrugged. "So what if I am? It doesn't matter to you. You're wasting your time here. I am freelance, remember? I don't have to obey anyone's orders, don't have a boss I report to, and if I choose not to continue with this case, then I do. That's not something you can change."

"You sound like such a—" Reynolds broke off, gave him an angry look. He turned away again. She moved in front of him, grabbing hold of his shirt. He reached up to take her hand off because she was not going to drag him anywhere. Katya bumped his legs, knocking him forward at the same moment that Reynolds yanked him toward her.

He knew what it was a second before it happened—a repeat of the moment in front of the press—a moment he had not expected to happen twice and not now, of all times. She still tasted of fire and spice. He forced himself away from her, tripping backward over the leopard. "Katya."

The leopard purred with contentment. He frowned at her. Reynolds looked at him. "Still see me as that woman from your past?"

"No—I—No, but that doesn't change—"

"Your cowardice?"

He glared at her. "I am *not* a coward. There is a difference between cowardice and awareness of my limitations. I told you before that I knew them. That—That only confuses the issue further."

"Maybe. But for that moment, you knew I was alive and here and fine. I am not the woman that died in front of your eyes. I won't be, either. I am the woman that is going to find this bastard and make sure he pays. Not that he's not already regretting this. When we find him, we'll nail him on the DNA your leopard got us—with her claws."

Randolph pulled himself up. "I told you to keep the leopard."

"Yeah, well, she has a mind of her own, and you know that better than anyone."

"This is a mistake."

"Finishing this case? No. We need this. All of us. And that bastard has to be stopped."

Persephone knew she'd won, but it didn't feel like a victory. Randolph was quiet. He flipped through the file without saying anything, and she didn't know that she was going to get him to talk to her again. He wasn't even talking to the leopard.

"Thoughts?"

Randolph ignored Marciano, tapping his fingers on the table. She exchanged a look with Marciano, who shrugged and shook his head. It was a mood. It would pass. Hopefully, at least. She was hoping that he'd snap out of it soon. It wasn't that she thought he'd just get over his past and the nightmares that lingered there, but she did believe he was the type that fought past them. He'd been determined to do it before—it was only what happened to her that made him change his mind. Well, her and the leopard.

"Everyone knows that he was injured when Katya saved me. Maybe that's enough. Maybe it means someone will notice and turn him in," Persephone muttered, reaching for her coffee. She sighed. "I wish I'd gotten something clearer than the damn baseball cap."

"Stop blaming yourself. As for someone else noticing, I doubt it. He is too solitary for that."

Persephone looked at Randolph. "Is he now?"

Randolph nodded with conviction. He put the file down. "He thinks he's in control again. Yes, he beat that woman as well, but he did it on purpose. He turned it into a part of his ritual. His MO. He believes this will obscure what this means to him."

"The fact that they have the wrong face, that they're not the woman he wants."

Randolph rose. The leopard tried to follow him, but he motioned for her to stop with his hand. He started to pace, agitated. "He still can't get what he wants, but he... I believe he's starting to enjoy killing."

"What makes you say that?"

"He almost took you."

Persephone shrugged. "I was in his way."

"But not his type. Not the proxy he needs. It would have been enough to incapacitate you and leave you there. He didn't have to take you. He's devolving fast," Randolph went on, making her want to shudder. It was hard not to be at least a little bit frightened by the discussion of her possible fate. She wasn't a fool. She knew that she could have been another one of the man's victims. It was only because of the leopard that she wasn't.

"What are you saying, then, Randolph? What are you thinking? That he walked away from being mauled by a leopard and picked up someone else already? Shouldn't what Katya did buy us a couple days at least?"

Randolph put a hand to his head. "You'd think so, but I doubt it. He has a taste for this now, and he wants to do more. He wants the woman that rejected him, and now that he's been stopped—temporarily—he's even angrier than he was."

"You think he'll make another attempt on Reynolds then?"

Persephone shook her head. "We just established that I'm not—"

"He will. You can't be allowed to get away from him. It undermines him, and he does not—*cannot*—accept anything that undermines him, not now. This thing goes back to a rejection that emasculated him. That same emasculation is what he's been fighting against, what he's hurting these women to prove. He's the type of rapist that does it to feel powerful, to feel like a man. You getting away from makes him... impotent all over again."

"Now you want me under protective detail?"

Randolph shook his head. "No. Now I want to make you a target. Deliberately."

Chapter Eleven

"You're kidding, right?"

"I'd like to be. I don't want to do any of this. You brought me back here, and I'm giving you another insane idea, and you're actually looking at me like you'll use it—that's the truly frightening part," Randolph said, pacing. His head was throbbing, and he could not stand the light and noise. He shouldn't have come back. He was hurting, and even if he hadn't been, he couldn't think straight.

"I think you've had enough for a while," Reynolds said, getting to her feet. "How long have you been fighting that migraine anyway?"

"Don't know. Not sure any of them have actually stopped," he admitted, sitting down again before Reynolds could touch him. Katya came over to him, putting her head in his lap. He ran his fingers through her fur and sighed. "Do we have a list of recent deaths in the area?"

"What do you want that for?" Marcie asked. Then he shrugged. "Hell, if it backs us off the idea of using Reynolds as bait, I don't care. I get why you'd point it out, and it might even work, but the cost—even just emotionally—is too damn high. For both of you. No, all of you. The damn leopard would never let it happen."

Katya lifted her head and hissed at the other man, and Marcie shook his head. "You know what I mean, cat. You'd get hurt again."

She blinked in that way of hers, and Marcie rolled his eyes. Randolph reached for his water. He could use something with caffeine to help with the headache, but he didn't feel up to getting a soda out of the machine. Reynolds looked at the cat for a moment. "Does she know how to work a vending machine?"

"Better than a few humans I know," Randolph agreed. "Still, I wouldn't make her do it right now. She's injured."

"No, I wouldn't. It just crossed my mind because—Well, I'll be right back," Reynolds said as she dug a couple of dollars out of her purse. "Marciano? He wants the list to see if we can find the overbearing mother or grandmother from his theory, the one whose death may have been the catalyst, 'freeing' this bastard to start this reign of terror he's got going now."

Marcie nodded. "Right. Makes sense. You still on that other theory, too? The one about her sister?"

Uncomfortable with his latest thoughts on that subject, Randolph shrugged. "I told you already. My judgment is flawed and compromised, and you're going to have to take anything I tell you with a great deal of salt."

"Agreed. Still, we *do* need you on this as much as you need it."

"You don't."

Marcie gave him a look as he took out his phone. *"Dita belle, amore,* can you look something else for me, perhaps? Oh, you know I adore you. And Randolph thanks you, too. No, no, he's not that good, but he's here, so that's something."

"Go to hell, Marcie."

"See? Told you. Yes, I need a search on recent deaths in the area. Older women, ones that left a son behind," Marcie began. He looked at Randolph. "What else?"

"Only child—or only surviving child. Inherited at least a minor estate involving a house. Could be a mother *or* a grandmother. Age range is somewhere between twenties and forties—I lean toward early thirties because of the other theory, but you can keep it wider for the search. House and vehicle registration in the woman's name and... this guy's never been married, never got close. Employed, but not in any kind of management position, no authority. Probably white collar pencil pusher kind of thing. The brunt of office jokes and that sort of thing..."

Reynolds set an open soda can down in front of Randolph, moving over to her board to add in the things that Randolph listed off. She stepped back with another frown. Randolph looked at her as he picked up the can. "What? You have something?"

She rubbed her shoulders. "You said this guy had no record?"

"Most likely he doesn't, but if you have something that would contradict it, don't hold back just because of my theories. Remember who's talking here."

She shook her head. "First thing we did was look into local sex offenders and eliminate them. You think he moved back in? Do we need to do another check of the registry? If there was an inheritance, then yes, he could have moved back and we might have missed that the first time..."

"You getting all this, *dita belle?*" Marcie asked his wife, smiling. "Yeah, I know, you're good. Why do you think I always call you even when I should deal with the locals?"

Randolph closed his eyes, trying to ride out the pain. It was getting worse. He knew he should say more, but he had to force Katya out of his lap and reach for the trashcan, emptying out his stomach.

"Okay, that is it. You're done for now," Marcie said, ending the call to his wife. Randolph nodded, unable to argue. He'd have to sleep this one off for a while. "We've got this, okay?"

"The leopard goes with Reynolds. Everywhere. No arguments. She doesn't leave her side."

"Randolph, I don't need the leopard—"

"Katya, you stay with your detective, yes?" Randolph asked, getting a purr from the cat. "Good. Very good."

"You look terrible," Lillian fussed as soon as she saw them, and Persephone almost smiled as she saw her mother taking charge of Randolph. Marciano thought it was amusing—he had a wide grin on his face despite the glare Randolph managed to send his way. Katya didn't seem bothered by Lillian taking over. She might even have been purring. "There. You lay right there and stay put. You're not moving."

This time Persephone did laugh, and her mother turned to her. "Oh, I wouldn't get so smug just yet, Persephone. You should be in bed, too."

"Mom, I'm fine. Randolph has a migraine, but I don't, and we need to keep working."

Lillian gave Randolph another push to keep him in place, and he tried to glare at her before closing his eyes again. Lillian shook her head, grabbing hold of Persephone's arm and almost dragging her over to the other bed. "You barely got out of the hospital, and I am not letting anything else happen to you. You will stay right there until *you've* gotten some rest, too."

"I don't need to stay here. I need to get out there and find this guy," Persephone objected, starting to get up again. Her mother pushed her down. "Mom—"

"You act like I'm expecting you to share a bed or something."

Persephone shook her head, grateful for the fact that Randolph was already out even though Marciano—right now was a moment where he deserved the 'Marcie' name he hated so much—laughed and grinned at her. This was ridiculous. Despite the leopard and a couple of kisses that were not done for any romantic reason, she and Randolph were not in a relationship. That wasn't going to happen, either. He was a good profiler, but he would move onto other consulting work, taking the leopard with him, and Persephone's life would go back to normal. That was fine by her.

"That is *not* the issue here because I am adult enough not to molest Randolph while he has a migraine, unlike the thoughts I'm sure are running through *your* head right now, Mother, but not only am I not a child to be put to bed, I am—"

"You're not working now. Period. You each have your own bed, and you're going to get some rest. Your leopard can lay here in between the both of you and get some rest as well," Lillian insisted, going to the closet. She pulled out an extra pillow and blanket, putting them on the floor for Katya. "Anything else you need, sweetie?"

The leopard rubbed against Lillian's leg and purred, voicing her approval before settling down on the pillow. Persephone rubbed her head. Even her mother had accepted the leopard—it helped that Katya had saved Persephone's life, but still... It was rather strange to see her mother so comfortable with a big cat like that.

Marciano thought the whole thing was hilarious, and he was still laughing. She gave him a look as she got up again. She didn't care what her mother said. Persephone had too much to do to stay in one place. She got halfway across the floor and Katya rose, blocking her path with a growl. Persephone sighed. "Cat, I'm fine."

Marciano shook his head. "That is so not a battle you'll win. Just accept it and get some rest. I'll let you know if we get anything—and trust me, this is just a sign that my wife is being very thorough. I expect to be more than a little impressed when she calls me back."

Persephone sighed again. Her mother touched her shoulder. "Please. You may as well take the time. If not for you—then for me and the leopard."

Katya swatted her pillow, getting in a playful mood, looking innocent and adorable as she did, and Persephone knew she'd never win—or forgive herself if anything else happened to the leopard. She sat back on the bed and waited, watching the cat play for a moment while her mother left with Marciano.

"I thought about pointing out that you never sleep more than four hours and would therefore wake quickly, but I doubt that was something you wanted your mother knowing."

Persephone nodded. "Yeah, she doesn't—I'm sure she suspects, but she doesn't need to know. Thought you were already out, Randolph."

"Too much noise."

"Not anymore," she disagreed, laying back on the pillow. It was too quiet in here without him talking, with just the sound of the leopard's purr and Persephone's own breathing.

"Good lord, woman, if I'd known you were going to scream like that, I would never have let them bully you into staying in here," Randolph muttered, putting a hand on his head as he eased himself up. He couldn't help grimacing as he crossed the room over to where Reynolds was still caught in the throes of whatever plagued her sleep. Katya had climbed up next to her, but it didn't seem to be enough. "Reynolds?"

Katya bumped him, and he gave the cat a dirty look. She opened her mouth and bared her teeth, and he frowned. Oh, hell, there would be no separating the leopard from the woman. A shame—he had grown rather fond of the cat. Still, perhaps Katya was the type that moved from person to person, the one that needed her most. Randolph had to face his demons here, and when he did, there would be no real reason to keep the cat around.

"Persephone?" he asked, keeping his voice quiet, combing back some of her hair as he spoke. He wasn't sure how to reach her—Katya should already have done that. He took hold of her hand, wincing as he saw the bruise on her wrist, much darker than it had been before. Her assailant had done his best to break that, hadn't he? "Love, you need to wake up now. He's not there. He can't hurt you."

Reynolds struggled a bit more, and Randolph looked at the cat. "Come on, lick her face. You do it to me."

The leopard shoved him with her head again, and he couldn't help frowning. "Why is this all up to me? I'm no better, and you know it."

Katya rose, put both of her front paws on him, and pushed him right on top of the woman. Persephone's eyes flew open and she looked up at him, struggling to control her reaction. "I must apologize. Katya seemed to feel this was a situation where a group hug was in order. Katya, please let me up now."

The leopard purred, licking his ear and making him grimace. He realized that Reynolds was still shaking, and he adjusted his position as best he could, adopting a low tone and spouting a bunch of soothing but pointless drivel until she seemed to calm down.

"I never scream."

"You did, but do not think I would hold that against you. You saw me beg—I assure you, there were ones where *I* screamed, as unmanly as that might be. Katya, you've made your point. I don't think that Reynolds needs to be crushed under nearly four hundred pounds of cat and man any longer."

Katya licked his ear again, and he reached up to wipe it off as he sat up again, relieved of the cat's weight. "That is disgusting. You know I hate that, and yet you persist in—"

He broke off as he heard Reynolds laughing. After her nightmare, he supposed that she *could* use the laughter, even if it was at his expense. She sat up and rose, going to the window. She patted her pockets down and let out a curse. "I don't have my phone."

"You did get knocked on the head and spent a day in the hospital. You should be taking it easy. And yes, thank you for the look—I am aware that I'm not much better, but I *did* try to walk away from this. You all dragged me back instead."

"You need this. We all do," Reynolds said, rubbing her arms as she shook her head. "I don't scream. I don't dream—"

"You rarely hit REM sleep, so you wouldn't dream," Randolph interrupted. "The fact that you apparently slept a lot later than that this time probably owes a lot to your injuries, and a nightmare is more than understandable given that you were attacked the other night. You know that I have not lost mine, and that incident was years in the past. Yours is far more recent, and the mind will replay it. Especially since you would be looking over it for anything you could use to stop him from hurting someone else."

She sighed. "I don't... I didn't get anything out of that, though. All I did was torment myself for no good reason. I actually made it worse than it was."

Randolph rose and went to her side even as Katya reached her. Reynolds ran her fingers through the leopard's fur, and he put a hand on her arm, keeping his touch light and gentle. "Our minds tend to play the *what if* game over and over. We have to know what we could have done differently, and even if there isn't something—if... no matter how many times we try to say there wasn't anything that could have changed, we stubbornly refuse to believe it. We try and find that one thing... And when that scenario plays out, sometimes it doesn't help... It's far worse."

"That's your experience talking, isn't it?"

"Yes."

"What do you think you could have done differently? Other than not get hit over the head?"

"Used my brain, for one thing, turned my usual skills of observation against him and talked him down somehow instead of begging him to let her go," Randolph answered. He closed his eyes and tried to ignore the memories that wanted to take control, push the screams and pleas out of his mind and make the pain stop.

"I'm not her."

"I know that. Don't think I don't. There are dozens of differences—that man's type was brunettes... teenagers or close to it—and her voice was much higher than yours. Her eyes were brown and then dead and lifeless. She had some kind of perfume that makes me gag whenever I smell it. She was tan and athletic and... She's gone, and you're not."

Reynolds shivered, and Randolph was startled by the realization that his arms were around her. He tried to back away and fell over the leopard again. He glared at the cat from the floor. "Damn it. Are you trying to get me killed, Katya?"

Katya blinked like she didn't understand what he was asking. Reynolds shrugged and sat down next to him. "Maybe she thought it was a group hug moment again."

Randolph shook his head. "I... I shouldn't have touched you."

"You still win the case for sexual harassment, remember?"

He sighed, lowering his head. "That's not... It is a disservice to the women we are here to help, being this... distracted and unfocused. I had something back at the station, but my head wouldn't let me pursue it, and I don't know what it was anymore. I should give everything I have to a man I worked with at Quantico—I hate him, he's more pretentious than I am with my accent and 'the third' tacked on to the end of my name, but he did train me, and he knows this stuff better than I do."

"I don't want to deal with anyone more pretentious than you."

Randolph smiled a little.

169

"Here. And you're going to eat that, no excuses."

Persephone rolled her eyes at her mother's fussing. "Only if you give me back my phone. Just because Randolph took it once does *not* mean that you get to start doing that. I need to work. I have to find this guy before he hurts someone else."

Lillian sighed. "I really—I know why you need to do that, but—I can't help worrying about you. I want you to take it easy. You were hurt, and don't think for a minute I've forgotten what you looked like when I first walked into that hospital room."

"No, I get it, that will haunt you for the rest of your life," Persephone agreed, annoyed. It wasn't like she didn't know the effect that would have on her mother or that she thought her mother should just be *okay* with what happened. Persephone was not okay with what happened, so why would her mother be? It wasn't like that had been good or that it didn't hurt and it even scared her a little. She was not over what happened—she just channeled it better.

"Ladies," Randolph intervened, putting a hand to his head. "Can we please keep the voices to a minimum if we must argue? I do not think I shall be rid of this headache any time soon, and as that is the case, I must ask for as much consideration as is possible."

"Yes, sorry, Randolph," Lillian agreed. She crossed back into the kitchen and filled him a cup of coffee. "Caffeine helps, doesn't it?"

"It can."

"What about those pills that Marciano brought you?" Persephone asked, picking up her fork and starting in on the eggs as she watched him rub his head. He needed more of a break. She would have regretted bringing him back if she thought he'd do anything *other* than torture himself while he was gone. He'd been at the site where his worst nightmares had happened, the memories he couldn't escape, and that was just—he'd been punishing himself whether he admitted that or not.

"They're to help prevent them, not deal with the pain when they're already here. That's an entirely different set of drugs, and if I take the ones that really work, I may as well write myself off for the rest of the day—because they work by knocking me out cold."

"Nice."

He gave her a slight shrug. "The pain is usually much more tolerable, and admittedly—I have been off the preventative pills for some time now. The chaos of changing jobs and insurance and homes made the prescription something that was easily forgotten."

"Yeah. How long have you been living out of your car anyway?" Persephone countered. Randolph froze, and she folded her arms over her chest. "You're not the only one who can make observations, Randolph. I can read between the lines, too. The leopard cost you several jobs in a row, and it's not like you could keep an apartment with a leopard—not easily, at least. How long?"

"Only a few weeks. This... This is not about the money, though. I need it, yes, but I do not... It's not... not the reason I came back or even the reason I came here in the first place."

"I know."

He lowered his head, putting it down on the table. Persephone reached across the table and touched his hand. He didn't look up, but she felt him squeeze it back. She looked up at her mother's step in the doorway. Persephone put a finger to her lips, and Lillian pointed to the stairs. Persephone shook her head, but she heard the leopard purring.

"You're welcome here as long as you need," Lillian told Randolph, setting a water glass and two pills next to it on the table. "Even after the case is over. I've got plenty of room, and the leopard is a hero around here."

Randolph looked at her. "Mrs. Reynolds—"

"Lillian."

"Mom—"

"The leopard agrees," Lillian said with a smile, patting Katya on the head before she returned to the kitchen.

Persephone winced. "You know you don't have to stay here."

Katya growled. Randolph sighed. "I don't think I have a choice, actually."

Chapter Twelve

"It's just an empty nest thing. With my brother across the country, my sister overseas, and my father gone, the house must seem... lonely. She works, but it's probably not enough to keep her busy, never seems to be, at least. She's always butting into my life. Give her an inch, and she takes a mile, and so I didn't—I really had no intention of letting this thing—you staying with her, I mean—go this far. It was just supposed to be a way to feed the leopard and occasionally change clothes. She'll take over your life if you let her, though," Reynolds said, shaking her head. She opened the door to her apartment and stepped inside. "Hence my need for... this, such as it is."

Randolph gave her a slight smile. She was, once again, embarrassed by the state of her home, but it did not bother him. He was the one who lived out of his car, after all. "Everyone needs their own space. A place to breathe."

"What is that look for?"

He'd been caught. Shrugging in apology, he tried to find the best way to say it. "Just... puzzling over you staying close when your siblings seem to have gotten as far away as they could."

"Oh, you know... Smaller city, lack of opportunities. They needed to move on to do the things they wanted to do, meet the people they were supposed to marry, and have the life they wanted. That's how it works sometimes," she answered with a shrug. He watched her for a moment. "Stop staring at me like that, Randolph. I am not a... puzzle to take apart and analyze."

He sighed. "I'm not taking you apart—I suppose I *am* analyzing you, a little, but I do that. Not every single little thing, no, but I didn't—I find their behaviour suggestive of running and yours... displays a greater sense of responsibility. It's your choice of vocation *and* the fact that you stayed close when everyone else left, as much as you get irritated with your mother's interference in your life."

Reynolds reached up to touch her stitches. "I don't know that I'm all that... Okay, that's not a puzzle look. That's something else."

Randolph looked down at the leopard. "I have no idea what these looks I keep giving her are. I suppose you know, Katya? Of course you do. You know everything."

The leopard licked his hand, and he grimaced. Reynolds laughed. "I'm going to shower and change. You think that you can make us a bit more coffee—or tea, I suppose—while I do that? Then you can take your turn if you want—I notice you didn't do that while we were at my mother's—are you afraid of her... nosiness, by any chance?"

He shook his head. "No. Just... not a fan of cold showers and heat aggravates my migraines. I should have grown more... accustomed to the cold ones, but it's not always an issue, so..."

"It is today."

He made a face. She smirked and walked away, leaving him to shake his head as he went into the kitchen. He didn't think it was that bad—and he certainly hoped that it wasn't—but she was most likely giving him a hard time. He supposed that he would need to clean up as well, though he was more looking forward to seeing what she did than his own necessary cleansing.

Katya bumped his leg, and he looked down at her. "We fed you already. No complaining."

The leopard knocked him into the counter this time, and he sighed, looking back at her. "What? This is getting very annoying, and I have no idea what you want. Sometimes I wish you could talk so that you could just spit it out."

Katya walked away from him, and he frowned when she did. "I'm not following you. I have this strange feeling you're trying to lead me into her shower—and that is not funny."

The leopard stopped and looked at him. He nodded. "Yes, she's a beautiful woman, I am aware of that, but that is not where this is going, thank you very much, cat. You can stop trying to point it out now. And you would only have made things very awkward. Not helpful."

Katya blinked. He studied the leopard for a moment. "You want to keep her, don't you? What if I said no?"

Katya growled, showing her teeth. He folded his arms over his chest. "I see. And if I say that you have to pick one of us?"

Another growl, more teeth. He shook his head. "No. Pick. I am not staying here. So if you want the detective, you have to stay with her. That's how it works. You don't get us both. And that is the end of this discussion. I am not marrying the woman simply because you think you want to keep her."

The leopard blinked, and he turned his back on her, going to the sink. He would not let the leopard control him like this. Yes, she *had* chased off the last woman in his life, and that had made him angry enough, but Katya did not get to pick who he dated and who he didn't. Reynolds could have the leopard. Katya was far more trouble that she was worth.

"Is your head bothering you again?"

"No."

"Well, you're... snippy," Persephone pointed out, because he had been ever since she got done in the shower. He did his best to avoid looking at her, took his own shower—he'd surprised her by taking a long one after his complaints about the water temperatures—and then when he got done, he hadn't said anything to her, not on the way back to the car, not in the car, not unless she asked a question. He'd kept his answers short and for the most part ignored the leopard as well. "What is going on?"

Randolph got to his feet and went over to her board, and Persephone shook her head. She knew he had a tendency to get caught up in whatever theory or memory was weighing on his mind, but she was sick of this. She didn't like being ignored. "Randolph—"

"Look, I know we don't have anything new, *amico,* but don't take that out on the ladies. You know how it works—the theory doesn't fit, so you start over again. You take the parts that do work and build on them. So we can't find a recent death that fits your theory. We don't stop looking."

"We could be dealing with a Norman Bates situation," Persephone offered, and Marciano smiled at that one before giving his friend a worried look. Persephone shrugged as the agent turned to her. She had no idea where Randolph's head was at the moment, but it didn't seem like a good sign that he snapped at the leopard. "Not even a little amusing, Randolph?"

"It's not that unlikely, actually," Randolph said, picking up the marker and underlining the baseball hat note. "You said you only noticed the hat when he attacked you."

"Yes. I know—all the training and observation skills went right out the window because all I could think about was how much my head hurt and how I couldn't breathe and that he was trying to get the gun out of my hand. I didn't get anything but the damn hat, and it pisses me off. Maybe we should have Katya check the mug shots again."

"If you want," Randolph muttered. The leopard went over to him, and he shook his head, trying to shove the cat away from his legs. "No. Stay away from me."

"Damn, Randolph. What did the leopard do? You're not usually like this with her."

"This because she tripped you earlier?" Persephone asked, not liking it any more than Marciano did. Randolph's headaches were one thing, and if he admitted that was what was setting him off, they could drop it, but the way he was acting right now was not like him, even if he was more than a bit screwy to begin with. "Come on, I think you can forgive her for that already."

"Not letting my life be ruled by the bloody cat," Randolph insisted. He shot Katya another dirty look and went back to the board. "The baseball hat—it's all you noticed."

"Yes, we went over that already."

"But *why?* Was the hat all that distinctive?"

"He was smacking my head into the back of a building and choking me at the same time, so I have no idea. It didn't have anything on it. Not a logo or a slogan, just an ordinary stupid ball cap, okay?" Persephone's voice almost reached a shout, and Marciano touched her shoulder. She shook him off as Katya came back to her side, giving Randolph a hiss. If he was trying to push the leopard away, he was doing a good job of it, but Katya wasn't the only one getting caught in whatever this damn mood was.

"Exactly," Randolph said, turning around. "We missed the point. The hat isn't special."

"Uh... What? You're all over the place right now, and I haven't been able to follow you. I just think you're—frankly, you're pissing me off."

Marciano laughed. "Yeah, it works that way sometimes. What are you getting at here? Something useful, I hope? I mean, I got them redoing canvases and upping patrols, but without something to actually go on here—"

"Why does he wear the hat?" Randolph interrupted. Persephone frowned again. "Typical reasons—promotion of a favorite team or business or branch of military service, that sort of thing, yes? Or vanity. A lack of hair."

"Or they like the fit of the thing. You aren't going to get anywhere with this. He's doing it to obscure how he looks. I didn't get hair color—just a dark hat—and the same with Mandy. That's all we know. He probably wasn't even wearing the same one in that alley."

"No, I agree with that, but... He didn't wear glasses, did he?"

"Well... No, but he wouldn't have when I met up with him because it was dark out. He would have been suspicious enough in the alley, but dark glasses? Asking for it, really."

Randolph nodded. "I agree. Again. Still... what if the reason he needs to obscure his head has nothing to do with the letter jacket or athletics of any kind as might have been suggested by their combination?"

"As in he's bald? What good does that—It doesn't really help, okay?"

"A scar. I think he has a scar. On his head. A very noticeable one that no one would forget if they saw it," Randolph finished, and Marciano shrugged in acceptance when he was done. Persephone rubbed her forehead, wondering why he couldn't have just said that from the beginning.

"Even with the idea of a scar, we don't know what it is, so it doesn't help," she reminded him, and he frowned this time. Poor man. After all that fuss, it was not the revelation he'd expected it to be. He was suffering from an inflated sense of his own ego at the moment.

His phone rang, and he flinched as he reached for it. Okay, so his head hurt, too, which explained part of his mood, at least. Persephone reached for her water and took a sip, going for a couple of painkillers to add to it. The area around her stitches ached—and itched—which was wonderful, really.

"Yes, that is the rumor," Randolph agreed, moving away from the board. "Very amusing. You know as well as I do that Katya would rather bite you than be your mascot. No, I did not tell her to—she disliked you long before that, and I am not that petty. A consultation over the phone? You know it doesn't work that way."

Persephone shook her head. "I suppose it's good that he's developing some business."

Marciano snorted. "Not if that's who I think it is. Yeah, it is, isn't it, Katya? Damn it."

"What?" Persephone asked as Katya growled. Whatever this was, it could not be good. The leopard was already kind of ticked at Randolph, and he was angry with her for some reason, so this was going to get ugly in a minute.

"I don't know what makes you jump to the conclusion that they're related. You are so paranoid, you do realize that, don't you? Yes, you are, Ashley, and no, I am not just saying that because you were jealous of a bloody leopard. It's not related, and unless you can prove it—" Randolph stopped, pinching the bridge of his nose. Katya jumped on him, knocking him down and taking the phone out of his hand. He glared at her. "You know, I know you hate her, but that could have been a job for me, and I don't appreciate you screwing up *another* one."

Katya spit out the phone, looking smug. Persephone looked at Marciano. "The ex?"

Marciano watched Randolph get up and walk away from the leopard, heading for the door. "Yeah. She's SAC—that is, she's got her own office where she acts like the damn queen—and while none of us liked her much, he did. Very nearly married her. The leopard got in the way, though."

Persephone looked at the leopard. "Wait—No. That cat is *not* matchmaking anyone here. It's not happening. I'm grateful, really, and I know I owe you my life, Katya, but that does not mean—It doesn't mean *that*. No. I'm not even going to think about that. What I want is a way to catch this bastard. That's it. That's all."

"Reynolds," Marciano began as she rose, and she stopped to look at him. "Could you... possibly try and get him back in here? I told you—he *did* care about Ashley, a lot. Every time she calls, she screws him over again, not that he doesn't have enough issues as it is. I'm not even allowed to discuss the woman with him, and you can bet the cat wouldn't go over well at the moment, either."

Persephone let out a breath. "I am so calling Angelina and having her kick your ass for getting me involved with any of this. This is not what I get paid for, and I don't like having to drag my profiler back repeatedly. You could have sent one with a lot less baggage."

"Randolph is the best profiler I know, and I'm not just saying that because he's my friend. The man is good. You haven't been able to see him at his best, but even off his game, you know he's helped a lot with this case. Same with the leopard."

"Doesn't mean I'm not calling her."

"I swear, if I have to drag you back to this thing again, I'm not going to bother," Reynolds snapped as she sat down next to Randolph on the small partition of grass outside the station. "This is really old, and if I don't care if you're good—I want a damn profiler that stays. I don't want one with a leopard or a bunch of issues. It would have been so much nicer if you'd been one of the more pompous assholes that come in, treat the local cops like complete morons, and then left. Yeah, I actually think I might have preferred that."

"I cannot say that I would blame you for that sentiment," Randolph agreed, not up to raising his voice. She had the hat on again, and he didn't know what it was about that look that appealed to him so much, but this was not the place or the time. "All I came up with was a damn scar, and you were right—we can't prove it. I don't know what I'm doing here anymore. I can't seem to get anything in order, and my leopard—now that's a joke. The leopard isn't mine. I'm hers as much as I bloody well hate being manipulated and controlled and stalked—my leopard has decided to ruin my life again. Absolutely perfect. The way I really *want* to work especially when it's something this important. This man is a killer but even if he wasn't—he needs to be stopped."

"Agreed."

"You know, I actually thought that the scar would trigger something for you."

"From when he attacked me that night? I didn't manage to knock his hat off, and the leopard may have mauled him and gotten his blood and skin as evidence, but all that gave us was what statistics were already telling us—a young white man."

Randolph nodded. "Still, I guess I thought it would have some kind of meaning for you."

She shrugged. "No. Well, I suppose I could make a connection, but I alibied that bastard out myself when this first started, and it wasn't him. A part of me wanted it to be, but I couldn't break his alibi for any of the abductions or dumps, and it's not him. Believe me, I've gone over that one repeatedly."

"You never mentioned him, though."

She turned away for a moment. "It's just an old vendetta."

"Jake Moore and his lies about you that lead to your isolation in high school?"

"Not him, but yeah, a different man along those lines," Reynolds said, looking away, her voice almost too quiet to be heard. "He doesn't fit your profile, either. His mother's alive, he has a girlfriend, and he doesn't work a white collar job. I just hate him, and I'd love it if it was him to give me an excuse to arrest him and lock him away for the rest of his life. I didn't say anything because we don't need my bias clouding the whole case. Like I said, I checked and rechecked his alibi. It's not him."

"My profile is not without flaws."

She laughed. "Don't. Don't give me another excuse to look at him. That will only end in a harassment suit."

"What did he do to you?"

"What did the woman on the phone—this Ashley person—do to you?"

"Convinced me to date her after I'd pretty much sworn it off—having a dead woman's voice in my head made that rather difficult, you understand—and then when she was up for a promotion, she gave them my theory on an old cold case, solved it, and got the job... without mentioning that it was my idea in the first place. Still, I'd have been almost foolishly willing to overlook that since she wanted us both to take the transfer and start a new life together. The vows and the proverbial house with the picket fence, the works. Only by then I had a leopard, and Ashley couldn't stand Katya's place in my life. Katya couldn't stand her. She tried to have the leopard put down as a dangerous animal, and that is the last I ever saw her. She was ambitious and driven, and that had always bothered everyone else, but that wasn't really an issue for us. It was what she did to Katya that proved unforgivable—and rightly so. I should have known Ashley would hear about me going freelance and think she could use that as a way to get me to work for her—and I *could* do that because it's not about the money or her—it's about the victims and stopping the people who hurt them. If she had a legitimate case, I would have agreed to work it, but it was just more lies and manipulation. Marcie says love works in strange ways. I go with the more cynical version— That it makes fools of us all. Me, of all people, I should have known better given what I do for a living."

Reynolds shrugged. "Just means you're human. We all make mistakes, and love is blind."

"This man... he hurt you badly, didn't he?"

She studied her bruise for a moment. "Typical story of my life— always defined by the way I look. He thought that I should roll over and thank my lucky stars that I had him because no one else wanted me. He thought it made him entitled to things I didn't feel like giving him. His attitude—Like I said, I want it to be him. It isn't."

Randolph shook his head. "You shouldn't have to settle for anyone, and the way you look doesn't define who you are because it is—you are a wonderful contradiction. The light hair, the cool eyes, the way you hold yourself... You seem as though you should be cold and aloof, but you are not. You're dedicated and driven and responsible, but it is more than that. I pictured a completely different person when I spoke to you on the phone, and as I told you before—you are not frosty."

She flushed, getting to her feet. "I don't want to have this conversation with you, Randolph. The lines are already—I just want to find the man that's hurting these women. Tell me we can do that, and we'll get back to work. If we can't, then... I won't drag you back again."

He stood, going over to her side. "Do you think I said what I did simply because I wanted to make you feel better?"

"I don't care what's going through that head of yours unless it relates to the case. We need to stick to that from now on."

"The leopard thinks I want you."

"She's a cat. A big one, and a very unique one, but still a cat."

"I didn't say that I find the way you look in the hat incredibly alluring."

"Well, don't. I look like a beekeeper or something."

"No, you don't," he insisted, pulling her close to him and helping himself to that spice again. He shouldn't—he had a list miles long why this was a terrible idea—but he could not stop himself. She had somehow gotten in past everything—the memories and the failures and even the leopard—and he did not want to let her go. He had to—there was no way they could continue like this, and he had known that before he started. He never should have taken this case no matter how desperate he'd been at the time. He shouldn't have come here. He forced himself to let go. "You do *not* have to settle, either."

She put her fingers to her lips, swallowing hard. "Damn it, Randolph. What the hell did you do that for?"

He considered making a joke about fair being fair, but that wasn't it at all. He couldn't say it was a fit of pique, either. He had known better and done it anyway. He owed her an explanation—he was not saying that the leopard was right, damn it.

"Forget it. Just—Don't do it again," Reynolds said, shaking her head as she walked away from him. "If you have something for the case... You can give it to Marciano."

"Persephone—"

"No. We have blurred the lines enough here, and it is past time that stopped."

Chapter Thirteen

"I'm going to talk to the women again."

"Take the leopard."

Persephone gave Randolph a dark look. "Are you kidding me? After that, you think you can—"

"You're still a highly visible target. You shouldn't go anywhere alone," Randolph countered. She could glare at him all she wanted. She could be angry. He didn't mind that. He didn't care. He was angry with himself. He was better than this, knew how to act professionally, and he knew he'd pushed when he shouldn't have.

"What, so I should take you with me?"

Randolph flinched. "You know I can't do that. Take Marcie. Take Batscher. I don't care. Just don't go alone. And the leopard is not enough, even if they have given you a gun to replace the one he took."

"I'm fine. And I'm sick of not acting like a damn cop."

"Reynolds—"

"The leopard's going with you. Take a female uni, too," Marciano ordered, interrupting them. Reynolds started to object again, but he held up a hand. "I don't even want to know at this point. I've got a couple agents coming in from the local office that I have to meet and brief, or I'd do it. I don't like the idea of upsetting them any more than Randolph does, but you're the one this guy would go after, and we are not giving him that opportunity, is that clear?"

"Yeah, crystal," Reynolds agreed. Katya gave Randolph a look, but he waved the leopard away.

"You're with her. You know that. You claimed her, so you protect her."

Reynolds gave him another look for that one, and Randolph ignored it as he started making notes. He had to finalize the profile before the other agents got here, and even more than that, he had to separate what was useful and proven from the tangents and sidelines his mind always got distracted by. Reynolds had been a part of that. His fascination with her was more than a little detrimental to the case. A part of him was still convinced that her sister played a part in this, and now... Now he had another theory that he liked even less.

"Okay, she's gone now. You want to tell me what that was about? That witch over in—"

"No. That's finished. I told you that. I took the call because she might have had work for me, and as much as I don't respect her as a person any longer, I don't—can't—turn down a legitimate offer. It wasn't one."

Marciano let out a breath. "So what is it, then? You say it's not the headaches, but don't insult me. I may not be as smart as you, may not have the fancy degree in psychology, but you're my friend, damn it. I know when something's wrong."

"My life is run by a big cat, Marcie. How much more wrong do you need things to be?"

"Not funny. I don't like it when you do that, and you've been on edge so much that I let it slide a few times when I probably shouldn't have, but you know better. Don't call me 'Marcie.' And spit it out, already, Randolph."

"I am going to do my job now. You will have a profile to share with the agents that are coming, and then I am recusing myself from this for good. I can't work like this."

"You can't work because you're attracted to the woman? Hell, *amico*, you're not dead. You are allowed to feel. The leopard likes her, so it's not an issue there. Not saying you go off and ignore what you're here to do, but you don't have to run from it, either. She's pretty. You two get along despite the fact that you overanalyze everything, and it's not a crime to be interested. She likes you back, if you're worried about that."

"I'm not."

Marciano studied him for a long moment. "This you blaming yourself for what happened to her again? You couldn't have pegged the alley he chose that night and kept her away from it. That's not how it works. You're a profiler, not a psychic. You can read things in evidence and infer from them and build a picture of who we're looking for, and sometimes it seems like something closer to magic, but we both know that it isn't. How many times have you pushed statistics on me when I question you? You have reasons for what you come up with—sometimes thin ones—and you have good instincts, too. Yes, I want you to do your job, but I am not sure why that means shutting yourself off completely."

Randolph rubbed his forehead. "I can't separate it right now. I want to tell you to drag Reynolds back because I'm convinced she's the key to it and that something *will* happen to her. It already has. It's—How do I know if that's instinct or just blind fear because I'm terrified of losing her? There is a reason for emotional separation, why partners aren't supposed to be involved, why military officers don't serve together or in the same chain of command. It's even a problem in workplaces where there are *not* lives on the line. That is why non-fraternization policies exist. We both knew before I came in on this thing that I was going to be fighting against my past and a lot of memories and trauma, and that alone is enough to where someone else would question my involvement in this, but if you add in her—us— then you may as well throw all of this out of the window and let that bastard walk."

"He is *not* walking. Sometimes there's something to be said for personal involvement. Sometimes it pushes us that much further, gives us that last piece we need. And as long as someone is around to temper your wild theories, I think you can handle this."

"We'll see if you still think that after I show you the latest one."

"I hate when you say that."

"How's your head?"

"Not great, to be honest," Persephone answered, sitting down across from Bethany Alda and trying not to let the itch get to her. She had ditched the hat in the car, not wanting the reminder of Randolph's words or actions earlier. He had thrown the whole thing off—it was easy to dismiss the times she'd kissed him because they weren't *that*. His had been... a declaration of intent. They both wanted a whole lot more than that kiss, and this was *not* the time for that.

"I heard this kitty saved you," Bethany said, reaching out to pet Katya. "Where were you a few weeks ago, huh, Kitty?"

"Working with the DEA, I think," Persephone answered. She wasn't sure where Randolph had been then or which part of the alphabet soup he'd belonged to at the time, but she did believe that he'd worked for nearly all of them before he showed up here. Angie had a good laugh about the suspect in some bust or other getting bit by the leopard—though she'd left out the fact that the profiler she was sending to Persephone *owned* the leopard. "She's a very busy cat. Hard to be in so many places at once, isn't it, Katya?"

"She keeps looking at the door. Something out there?"

"She belongs to the profiler we brought in, and he's not here, so she's torn. While I apparently have her protection, she wants to get back to him, too."

"Oh. Why didn't he just come then?"

Persephone did not want to explain that one. The real reason he wasn't here right now was because they'd kissed earlier. She had a feeling if not for their fight after that, he would have forced himself to go through the interviews so that he could stick close to her. "He didn't want to upset you."

Bethany laughed a little. "They had a guy doctor do the kit. Can't really get worse than that, can it? I need a cigarette. Do you mind? Will she? I can't—I don't know what I can tell you. I've tried, but I don't remember more than that. I don't... Nothing's come back to me."

The girl got up and dug her cigarettes out of her purse. Alda was a chain smoker, and Persephone hated the way she smelled when she left the girl's apartment, but the cigarettes did keep her somewhat calm. Persephone could deal with the smell. She glanced at the cat. Katya pushed her nose at the door.

"Guess that's a no from her, huh?" Bethany muttered. She put the lighter down. "Funny thing is that I was gonna quit before this happened. Now it's even harder to let go of."

Katya went over and licked Alda's hand. She forced a smile for the cat. "You have any new leads on the guy?"

Persephone didn't want to lie, but she knew they didn't have much. She needed to go talk to the family of the second dead girl, too, but she'd started with the live victims because she knew that the attack on her was another blow to everyone's morale. "Unfortunately, I didn't see much when he got me in that alley. A baseball hat. The profiler thinks our guy is using it to cover up a scar, and we've been going through a lot of leads, rechecking everything. They did get the feds involved, and there are a lot more people working on this case and hunting that man. Oh, and the leopard got her claws into him, didn't you, Katya?"

The leopard purred. This time it sounded smug. Bethany nodded in approval. "Good cat. Huh. A scar, you think?"

"Does that mean anything to you?"

"Maybe. Kind of remember weird skin when I was pushing at him, but you know, none of that is very clear because of the drugs. I don't know. Sorry. I wish I could tell you something that would let you get this guy for good but—Okay, what's with the cat now?"

Persephone frowned, looking over at the leopard. She'd gone to the window and was looking out at the glass. The officer that came with her moved to the door. "I'll check the lot again, but the patrol car outside would have notified us if anyone was out there."

"Shit," Bethany said, reaching for her cigarette again. "Tell me the cat's just being weird and that he's not out there waiting for me."

Persephone went over to the window. "I don't see anything. Katya, is it Randolph? Something's wrong with him?"

The cat dropped down from the window and started to pace. Persephone ran her fingers through the cat's fur, and the leopard stopped, putting a paw on her leg. "What is it? Another migraine?"

"The cat gets migraines?"

"No, but the profiler does," Persephone answered. She knelt next to the leopard. "I still don't know how to read your looks, not like he does. What is it?"

Katya leaned against her and closed her eyes, sliding to the floor. Persephone frowned. "This had better not be drama queen stuff, cat. We don't have time for that. And if you make me call him and upset Bethany, I'm not going to be happy."

The leopard bumped the pocket with her phone, and Persephone took it out. "Missed calls, huh? I suppose you noticed the vibrating when I didn't. Okay, fine, but the window thing? That was a bit much. You freaked everyone out. Go apologize to Bethany while I call BB back."

The leopard gave her another look, and Persephone shrugged, pushing her off toward the girl she'd scared for no good reason. "BB, if you called me to complain about the feds—"

"Called you 'cause something's up with *your* fed. Get back here as soon as you can."

BB hung up, and Persephone shook her head. She looked over at Bethany. "It's her owner. Not the man who hurt you. I'm going to leave Officer Remos with you for a while, though, as an extra precaution. And you, Katya, do not get to go on any more interviews."

The leopard just blinked at her.

"You have anything other than the picture to lead you to any of this?"

Randolph sighed, rubbing his forehead. He reached for the soda and shook his head. "I already told you that it was mostly just... instinct. I saw that picture, and I can't get it out of my head. If we were at the Reynolds' house, I'd be looking at it right now. It's there. Right there. The usual sunny blonde full of smiles right next to her awkward, pale sister who would give anything to escape from that picture."

"So? Most of us hate family pictures. And maybe she just didn't like being photographed. Some of us don't, you know. We're not photogenic. Not like you are."

"Screw you, Marcie. Just because that one modeling agency tried to recruit me during that case—"

"The same modeling company that was a front for a very expensive 'escort' service," Marciano interrupted, enjoying that memory way too much like always. Randolph's flustered refusals at the time had been an endless source of entertainment for the Italian. He would have thought Marciano would have been upset that his own native charm didn't get him any offers, but for some reason, Randolph was more of what they were looking for, though he could not say why. "That always gets this look on your face..."

"I have a headache. Can we get back to this so I can finish it and go?"

"Right. Back to the off-base theory. You sure you're not just drawn to the picture because you're in love with the woman?"

"Too soon to be in love with her, and I prefer her as she is now and with a hat, actually. It is not just that," Randolph disagreed, ignoring Marciano's smug look. Yes, Randolph had feelings for the woman. He admitted that. He admired her and thought her quite lovely, but that was not what drew him to the picture in her home. "I thought it was the contrast at first, the sharp difference, that she didn't belong, but she has features from both of her parents. And the family was close prior to her father's death. I believe that event scattered them, fractured them far more than any of them realize or care to admit."

"Probably, but I think you might be overanalyzing your girlfriend a little."

"She's not my girlfriend."

"The leopard seems to think so."

"I am not marrying the woman simply because the leopard picked her. That's not how it works."

Marciano grinned. "You have any idea what you just said? You're talking marriage. This is serious."

"Don't make me hurt you, Marcie."

The other man just grinned. "What? Come on, it's good. You deserve some good for a change. Things haven't gone that well for you lately, so... Embrace the good. Especially when the good is beautiful and has a gun."

Randolph picked up the board's eraser and threw it at him. "Focus, please. You're supposed to be deconstructing my theory, not my love life or lack thereof."

"Okay, so where were we? Right. You're convinced the new girlfriend's ex is the guy we're looking for? Is that what I'm getting from this?"

"No. I don't think she was ever dating the man. I think the guy was hung up on her sister."

"You lost me. Again."

Randolph gave him a dirty look. "If you would stop bringing my feelings for Reynolds into this, you wouldn't be confused at all. You're getting distracted. Now, if you wouldn't mind sticking to the topic for a minute, we can get through this."

"And maybe if you weren't so caught up in your past, you would know that this twisted theory of yours doesn't protect anyone. You're just blind to the facts because all you can see is what was and not what is."

Randolph grabbed the marker and threw it this time. It missed Marciano and almost took Batscher's head off. Marciano laughed, and Randolph grimaced. "Sorry. He's just being... right, as usual."

"You said I was right. This is a moment for the history books."

"Shut up, Marcie," Randolph said, but they were both laughing before he finished speaking. This was so typical of them it was no wonder the higher ups stopped assigning them together. They saw this and never thought they were doing their jobs.

"All kidding aside, you know it's not the same, right?"

Randolph picked up the eraser and set it back against the board. "It's more complicated than that. You know I want you to tell me I'm wrong, but I don't think I am, and that's what bothers me. I can see it so clearly..."

"Whoa, now I don't think—"

Randolph's head flared with a new, sharp pain, and he put his hands to his head as he lowered himself down, trying to push it back to a tolerable level. He felt a hand touch him, and he knew it was Marciano's, but he didn't see his friend when he looked up. *No, damn it, not now...* He couldn't do this now. He didn't have time for this.

Randolph heard the snap of metal and opened his eyes again. He didn't want to—it wasn't like he didn't still see the images that had been there before he passed out. They would never go away. He was face-to-face with the bastard now, and there was no getting away from him. "You didn't have to do that to her."

"Yes, I did. You know I did."

"There was always a choice—you chose *to do that. You could have let her go."*

The other man laughed, smearing blood on Randolph's face. "You know you wanted to be a part of this. I know you did. You want to touch her, don't you?"

"No!" Randolph shouted as the killer undid the shackle on his other wrist, pulling him away from the wall. "Let go of me! I'm not touching her! I'm not a part of this, you sick son-of-a—"

"Don't talk that way about my mother."

"If you loved your mother, how the hell could you do that to them?"

The blow that followed that question left him spitting up blood and teeth, and the rest of his stomach wouldn't be far behind it. He felt the man's hand grab his wrist, dragging him forward, almost yanking his arm out of the socket. *"You know why, shrink. You know me so well. You already have all the answers. Because we're alike, you and me. You understand me. Now touch her."*

"I'm not touching her. You should have let her go."

"You know why she had to die. And soon it will be your turn."

Chapter Fourteen

"All right, BB, where is everyone?"

"New feds went out to do everything we've done at least twice already a third time. Old feds... Not here," BB answered, not even looking at her. Persephone shook her head. This was not funny. He didn't call her down here and then blow her off like this.

"Where, then?"

"I don't know. All I know is that your fed had a major meltdown, and his friend couldn't talk him out of it. Kept saying something weird like he wasn't going to touch her, and no, I have no idea why. Left me to deal with the new feds, and they were your typical fed jerk types. Told you your fed was a lunatic," BB grumbled, reaching for his phone.

Persephone shoved the phone back onto the cradle. "Randolph worked a case like this where the rapist turned killer whacked him over the head with a shovel and made him watch as he killed another girl. He's not a lunatic. He has very legitimate post-traumatic stress. Still, he was fine when I left. What the hell happened?"

BB sighed. "I walked in on him and the other fed going back and forth over some theory. Your guy was saying that it had to be this way, and the other one warned him about getting too caught up in it because of his past—which makes a lot more sense now—and your guy snapped at him and threw the marker across the room. They both started laughing. I figured things were fine, but then he flipped his lid, and that is all I know. I swear. I tried calling you when he was weird, but by the time you got here, it was all over."

Persephone shook her head, taking out her phone. "Mom? No, I don't want lunch. Randolph and Marciano there?"

"No, honey, and you do realize it's actually more like dinner time, don't you?"

"Whatever. I'll call you later," Persephone muttered, hanging up again. "You have Marciano's number at the hotel or even just the hotel he's at?"

"I think you might just follow the cat. She seems to know where she's going."

"I was supposed to talk to the victim's family. I should be dealing with this, not trying to keep track of the damn profiler."

"So give him the cat back and work like a normal person."

"BB, the guy behind all this—a rapist and a murderer—got the better of me in an alley, hit me on the head, and would probably have killed me if not for the leopard, so I'm not supposed to go anywhere alone, remember? I left Remos with Alda because the cat freaked her out. I can't just leave the cat behind."

"Ah. You need a partner. Guess I can stand in for the Brit for a while. Let's go," BB said, grabbing his coat. Persephone rolled her eyes. She didn't want his company, and Randolph wasn't her partner. She had almost said to hell with having extra protection, but she couldn't shake off Randolph's words—she was the one woman that this bastard *couldn't* let get away. The others he'd used and discarded, but he didn't get to do what he'd wanted to do to her. The leopard had made sure of that. She wasn't crazy. She was aware of her limits, though, and this bastard had gotten too close before. That wasn't going to happen again.

"Something I should tell you, Reynolds," BB began as they reached the door and started for her car. The leopard waited next to it, her tail thrashing around in impatience.

"Oh, BB, if you've finally discovered you have feelings for me, I should warn you the leopard already claimed me."

BB rolled his eyes. "Not that. Look, I know we've never really gotten along all that well, and you don't think much of me, either, but I didn't... I haven't been pulling my weight on this case, and I know it. I didn't follow your lead or your orders, and I wouldn't listen to your profiler. So... I should apologize."

"Do it to the victims, not me."

"Uh, in case you've forgotten, you *are* one of the victims."

"Not a victim."

"What?"

"Survivor. I'm a survivor. Remember that," Persephone insisted. The leopard growled and jumped out the car's window, running up toward the door of a hotel room and scratching on the door. A minute later, the door opened, and Marciano smiled down at her, letting the cat into the room. He stopped and looked for Persephone, waving her in. She shook her head as she got out of the car. She supposed that she'd have to tell Marciano to keep the cat.

"Wait up, Reynolds," BB called, and she looked back at him. He was taking this way too far.

"I'll be fine with Marciano."

"Maybe I don't feel like waiting in the car," he said, shrugging as he followed her. She rolled her eyes as she moved past Marciano and into the room. "Man, you'd think that the government would spring for a better room than this."

"I'm on my own dime, and I could have stayed with family, but I had a feeling I'd need my own space," Marciano said, shrugging, looking around the room with its dated furniture, fake wood paneling, psychedelic print sheets, and shag carpeting. "'Sides this reminds me of home."

"Mrs. Marcie puts up with this?"

"No, so that's why he gets his shag carpeting fix on the road," Randolph muttered from the bed. Persephone folded her arms over her chest and shook her head. The leopard had climbed up next to him, and he was trying to keep her out of his glass.

"Self-medicating, are we?"

Randolph finished the drink. "Marcie declared me off the clock. You really want to make this an issue, Reynolds? I could have taken the other pills, but then I'd be out for more than a few hours. Besides, I keep trying to tell him that I'm done, but he's not listening."

"Done? Again? You're going to pull that crap, are you?"

Randolph dislodged the cat and went over to refill the glass. "The alibi is a lie. I don't care who lied for him—his mother or the girlfriend—but it was a lie and you knew it. You've known all along who this was and why he was doing it."

"What? I thought you were going off on the completely nuts theory that it was about my sister—"

"That was why he went there that day, maybe, but it wasn't—You said you never wore the sundresses, but that doesn't mean you didn't try them on, does it?"

"Don't do this, Randolph—"

"I *have* to. I have to get it out, once and for all. The whole thing," Randolph insisted. He took a sip from the drink, struggling with what he was trying to say. "He went there for Sarah, didn't he? He mistook you for her—with your back to him, wearing one of her dresses, one of the hats you hate so much on your head... He came there to tell her how he felt, but he told you. And when he saw it was really you, he got angry, didn't he?"

"Drop it," Persephone warned, shaking her head. She wanted to leave, right now, wanted to run. She wasn't sure why she stayed where she was. This was the last thing she wanted Randolph bringing up. "I told you that—"

"That you checked his alibi multiple times and wouldn't let the case get biased by what you knew because you're a good cop. I know that. Still, you were almost his first proxy, weren't you?"

She moved toward the door. "You and your damn theories—"

Randolph got there before she could. He caught her, putting his arms around her. "I'm sorry. I am so sorry that I—that you had to revisit these old wounds, but you can't ignore it."

"I didn't. I told you I checked. You really think I'd let him get away with it? Go to hell, Randolph."

Sarah had all the pretty clothes, Persephone thought, irritated, wondering why she'd ever offered to help her sister pack. Sunny was

out with all of her friends, like always, and Persephone was here, alone, again. She picked up the sundress that Sunny had worn to her graduation party and shook her head. She couldn't go out in the sun. Ever. She was the white queen. The frosty witch. That was what they all said. Stupid Jake Moore. She should punch him right in the face.

Her sister wouldn't be home for a few hours, and if Persephone put the dress in the box when she was done, Sunny would never even know she tried it on. Persephone wouldn't hurt anything if she did, and she was inside, so it wasn't like the sun could burn her in here.

She took off her shirt and pulled the dress over her head. It bunched up around her waist, so she unbuckled her jeans and stepped out of them, fixing the dress. Wait. One thing was missing. She went back to her own closet and grabbed her hat, twisting her hair up and putting the hat on her head. She went over to Sarah's dresser and picked up the lipstick, using the full-length mirror to apply it. Persephone never did this. This was Sunny's thing.

She gave the mirror a mocking kiss and froze when she heard someone laughing behind her. "You're so beautiful, Sarah."

Persephone flinched. She didn't want to hear this. She wasn't her sister. She started to turn around.

"Don't. I need to tell you something, Sunny—"

"She's not here," Persephone said, turning around and taking off the hat. "Thanks for mistaking me for her. It makes my day, but you

209

don't belong here, so you can leave."

"When will she be back?" the boy asked. She knew him. She went to school with him. He was one of Jake's friends, and he had no business talking to Sunny. She was older than him—and didn't even know he existed. "I wanted to show her my new jacket."

"I hate to break it to you, but Sarah wouldn't care. You might think you have a chance because she dated the football team and the baseball team and half the basketball team, but she isn't impressed by letter jackets anymore, if she ever was in the first place. Oh, and she's going to college. I'm in here packing up her stuff because she's leaving tomorrow."

"Shut up. You don't know anything."

Persephone frowned. How had he gotten in here, anyway? "Are you... her math tutor?"

"She likes me. A lot."

"Enough to give you a key to our house? No. Get out," Persephone ordered. "If you want to come back, you call her and make real plans, but this is my room, too, and I have every right to kick you out."

"Always the ice queen, huh? You looked almost human for a minute."

Persephone rolled her eyes. "I am human, you idiot."

"Today was supposed to be the day. Finally the right time. Had *the jacket, was gonna tell her how I felt. It was supposed to be the day."*

Persephone didn't care. This was her sister's mess not hers, and she didn't even think that Sarah had any idea that this guy was interested in her. She moved to the door and started to push him out. "I'm sorry, but you need to go."

He pushed her back, and she stumbled over the foot of Sarah's bed, falling on it. Persephone started to get up, but he was on top of her, trying to hold her down. "Get off of me."

"Why should I? It's not like anyone else wants you. I'm doing you a favor, Frosty," he told her, kissing along her neck, shoving the dress up her legs. She twisted in his grasp, trying to kick him off. Wait, this was Sarah's bed, and she'd been packing her sister's stuff. She knew that she'd dropped it on the bed... Where was it?

Her fingers found the statue—one of Sarah's many awards—and hit him with it as hard as she could. He cursed her, reaching for the hand that had the statue, but she hit him again, this time using the heavy marble end of it. He fell backward, and she kicked him the rest of the way off the bed. She held the statue as she moved to grab Sarah's phone, calling the police.

He started for her foot, and she screamed before she hit him again. This time he didn't move, and she forced back tears as she spoke to the operator. She shuddered, wondering if she would ever stop feeling his hands on her.

Chapter Fifteen

"I hate you. I don't care how you figured any of that out, but you—you've done enough. Let go of me," Persephone said, trying to get out of Randolph's hold. She didn't want him touching her. She didn't want to hear his voice or think about anything he'd dragged up from her past. "Randolph, I'm not kidding. I may have been injured the other day, but I am not going to stay here a minute longer. I don't care what kind of a migraine you had, or if you flashbacked earlier. I'll hurt you."

He shook his head. "I can't let you leave, not like this."

"Screw you. You come in here and pick apart people's lives like puzzles, and it's nothing to you, but it's everything to me, and you can't tell me that I was right and didn't break the alibi because none of those girls should have gone through that if that's true because I didn't stop at bashing him over the head. I called the police; I made sure that he got arrested. Now you're telling me I should have killed him, and I—"

"No, that is not what I'm saying, and one thing this is *not* is easy for me. I had a man hit me over the head with a shovel and make me watch him rape and murder a girl and then he tried to tell me I was just like him because I could profile him. He was going to add me to his body count, and I don't even know how I got away from him. I don't do this because it's easy or because I feel smug and superior when I take apart someone's life. Sometimes I use it as a defense, yes, but I told you—I can't get her screams out of my head. I saw that picture of your family, and I saw your sister was his type and... I knew he would go after you. He did, and I didn't—I hadn't even told you about that part of it... I'm not saying you should have killed him, though I'd gladly do it or let Katya do it after what he's done—not just to them but to you—and I can't let you become that woman in my head, Persephone."

She shuddered and leaned into him. They were both so broken that their screwed up little pieces might just fit together. He led her over to the bed and helped her to sit. The leopard came over to her and put her feet in Persephone's lap. Randolph started to get up, and the leopard moved so that she was holding him down as well.

"Cute, Katya."

"I want you to be wrong. I *checked* his alibi. Every damn time. After what he tried to do to me, I knew he was capable of it, and I kept going back with each new girl, but it was never him. And you were wrong about the inheritance and the girlfriend and the job—"

"I told you—not science. Not always exact. This is him, though. I know it, and you know it," Randolph said, combing through her hair.

214

"The way he reacted when you surprised him in the alley... I think he's been working up, not to confronting your sister, but *you*. The ultimate moment for him will be when he finishes what he started all those years ago."

"He's not touching me again."

"No. He won't. He won't get anywhere near you," Randolph told her, and the leopard purred in agreement. Persephone looked down at the cat and shook her head. She didn't feel any better. Now that he knew all that it just made things worse.

"Stupid skin condition... Damn ice queen thing..."

"You are beautiful and unique," Randolph insisted. "That was just an excuse for his inadequacy. For *all* of their inadequacies."

"Not frosty?"

"Fire and spice and extremely addictive," he told her, and she managed a smile. He touched her cheek, and she closed her eyes for a moment, thinking he just might kiss her again, and despite everything, she thought she wanted that. "We need a name, love, and then we'll match his DNA to what was under the leopard's claws and lock him away for a very long time."

"I'd rather just kill him."

"It doesn't make what he did or said go away."

"Randolph—"

"Don't think I don't know. The other man, the one that haunts me... I did kill him, somehow—I don't remember the details—but his voice is still there almost constantly. Hers is the only thing that drowns him out."

Persephone sighed, touching the button on Randolph's pocket and turning it in a half-circle for a moment. "What happened earlier? What did you see? Something about... touching?"

"He wanted me to touch her after he'd killed her. Thought I wanted to, that it made me a part of what he'd done. He dislocated my shoulder dragging me to her, promised to kill me, and... That's actually the most of that period that's come back to me."

She let out a breath. "Can we at least say the bastard resisted arrest when we go after him?"

"Only if the leopard gets to bite him."

"Oh, Persephone, come in, come in," the older woman welcomed Reynolds with a warm expression, not even asking her what this was about. She smiled, a bit sheepish, as she looked around her front room. "You'll have to excuse me. I haven't gotten much cleaning done today. My hip doesn't go like it used to."

The room was spotless, and the furniture was covered in plastic, well-preserved since before Randolph was born, but she continued to fuss about as she invited them to sit. Reynolds shook her head and took a spot by the door, refusing to sit down. Katya gave the woman a look and jumped right onto her couch, watching her like she just might attack the old woman. "Mrs. Haye—"

"I haven't seen your mother in forever, Persephone," Haye went on, picking up a doily and dusting under it. "How is she?"

"She hasn't talked to you since your son tried to rape me," Reynolds said, shaking her head in disbelief. It wasn't something Haye should have forgotten, but then she didn't seem to be all there at the moment.

"My son? Oh, if you're here to see him, you'll have to come back later. A shame. I never seem to have any visitors anymore. He's gone with his young lady friend. You know, I think that's getting very serious. You should have snapped him up when you had the chance, Persephone."

"What?" Reynolds demanded, shaking her head. Katya growled, getting down from the couch.

"Katya. Outside," Randolph ordered. She gave him a look, and he folded his arms over his chest. "No biting. Go."

The leopard gave him a sour look and bumped his legs as she walked out. He turned to Reynolds, but she jerked away from him when he tried to touch her. He sighed and moved over to stop the older woman's cleaning. "How long has your son been gone?"

"They've been looking forward to going away for so long... I can't remember when they left, though. Must have been a while. I can't seem to find my glasses. Have you seen them?"

"You're wearing them, Mrs. Haye," Randolph told her, and across the room, Reynolds grimaced, rubbing her forehead. "How long have you been off your medication?"

"I have medication?"

Randolph shook his head, turning back to the others. "I doubt he's been here since Katya mauled him, and if he's responsible for keeping her on her medication, she's been without it for a while. I don't think we'll get anything from her until she's been stabilized again."

Reynolds cursed and left the house. Marciano came over to him. "Go. We'll handle this."

"We don't actually have a warrant to search the house, and I think they'd argue that she's not competent to give permission, so don't get happy here. If we find anything, it'll get thrown out," Randolph reminded him and Batscher before he left.

He found Reynolds outside, kneeling next to the leopard. He approached her, slow so as not to startle her. "How many times was the old woman his alibi?"

"Twice."

"On her medication, I suspect she's quite lucid."

"Enough to piss me off, yes," Reynolds agreed. "What now?

Breaking a couple of his alibis doesn't mean we have enough for a search warrant, and if we say she gave us permission, it'll just get thrown out in court."

"I agree, but I know Marcie's devious enough to find a way around that. What concerns me is the fact that she thinks her son is on a trip with his girlfriend."

Reynolds frowned, getting to her feet again. The leopard gave her a look and started circling her legs. "Well, if he managed to fool her so far, hide what he is, I think she would have to know now."

"Reynolds, she's either helping him or she's dead."

"Helping him? Why would any woman do that?" Reynolds demanded, wrapping her arms around herself and shivering despite the heat. "I can understand him putting on an act for her—and he'd be convincing, I'm sure, because I never even knew he was the one helping my sister with her math classes so she could graduate—but going so far as to help him do that to other women? Why? How? How could *anyone* do that?"

"After years of abuse and psychological conditioning, things can get... warped. Or they can be twisted from the word go. Another argument about nature versus nurture that I do not want to debate at the moment," Randolph admitted, and Reynolds nodded. He reached to touch her shoulder and then changed his mind, cupping her cheek instead. "This isn't your fault. It's not like you stopped when his mother alibied him out. You kept checking."

Reynolds nodded. "I know, but it makes me so... If I could have found a way to stop him sooner..."

"He has probably been planning this a long time. The women he chose might have been just the opportunity that he seized, but getting back at you was probably a long term goal. He put things into place slowly, lining up the girlfriend and the exploitable situation with his mother, but he was very careful... It was something that was bothering me—the dual nature of it, the planning at war with the opportunistic parts, the lack of forensics and the care and time needed to assure that. Part of it felt like two different people—which could have been the girlfriend—or it was my inability to connect something or see beyond my own past."

"He's doing this because of me, because I stopped him before—"

"This isn't your fault," Randolph insisted. "You had every right to tell him no, and he did *not* have the right to take it from you. He had free will the entire time. No one *forced* him to try what he did with you or to rape and kill those women. It doesn't matter how much he thought he loved your sister or if you gave him a scar. He still *chose* to do that. He can try and excuse it all he wants, but it was still a choice. Taking the girls was an impulse, but he planned so much of the rest of it that there is no way he didn't know what he was doing or setting up. There was time to walk away, time to stop himself, and he chose not to. Hell, you gave him a way to stop every time you asked for an alibi. He could have turned himself in, but he didn't. We can only control ourselves, Persephone. You did your best to stop him, but in the end, it was still a choice he made."

She nodded, and Randolph forced himself to let go of her. "I have this completely inappropriate urge to kiss you at the moment."

She smiled a little, but it faded as her professionalism took over again. "We should go to his girlfriend's place, see if she's home, if she's talked to him, what her friends or family might know about this trip if it exists—and it shouldn't because I told him not to go anywhere—or if she's dead."

Randolph nodded. "I assume you know where she lives?"

"Yes," Reynolds answered. "I spoke to her a couple times. She refused to see me after that. Didn't want to hear that her boyfriend was a pervert. Said whatever issues I had with him, that was the past, and I needed to learn to let it go."

"Willful ignorance is probably the hardest to take. She should have known, but she refused to listen," Randolph shook his head, taking Reynolds' arm. "We need to grab Marcie at least, and then we'll go see the girlfriend. You're still up to this?"

Reynolds gave him a look. "Are you?"

"I thought we were going to have the leopard bite him if he's here. Why are we standing outside and letting Marcie do all the work?" Persephone demanded. She didn't get this, and she wasn't sure she liked the way that Randolph was acting at the moment. He'd stopped her, pulled her back before they went up to the girlfriend's house, and she'd figured it had something to do with the way the girlfriend had refused to listen, but now she wasn't sure anymore. "Randolph? Did you really think I'd take it too far and try and kill him while we were arresting him? Because I don't need you saving me from myself. I want to hurt this bastard, but I am not a murderer, either."

Randolph put a hand to his forehead, frowning, and she pulled on his shirt, trying to draw him back from wherever he was going. "Hey. If you're getting a migraine, tell me. If not... No flashbacks right now, okay? You need to stay with me. Or is it something else?"

"He's not here."

"Okay, yes, I kind of figured that, but I'm not sure what is bothering you so much. So he's not here. We didn't really think he'd make it easy for us, did we? He had a way to counter everything else, but he knows we've got him as soon as we test him against what we got from Katya's claws, so he had to run," Persephone said, shrugging. She didn't like the fact that the bastard was still out there, but she did like forcing him on the run, disrupting his sick game. "If we get his DNA from here or from his house, we can match it without him, and then we'll put his name and face up everywhere so that he has nowhere to hide, nowhere to run or turn, so he can't hurt anyone else. It's not ideal, I admit that, because I want to haul his ass in there myself, but I'll take what I can get. He's not rich. He can't just go get his face changed and hide again. He'll get caught."

Randolph let out a breath and looked into the distance. She gave the shirt another pull. "This is not the same as you moving onto another case. It's not like we've finished this. We'll put out the manhunt, and then we'll wait for him to think he can make a move on me because he'll have to try, and we all know that, too. The thing is, though, he has to go after a cop, and he won't get close. Not this time."

The haunted look in his eyes was getting to her. She looked down at the leopard, but the cat was focused on the area around them, almost looking right through Persephone. "Wait. Is he—You just said he wasn't here, but you're acting like you did in that alley when the kid was watching us. You think Haye is watching now? Or is that kid back? I know he probably made bail or something stupid like that, and I haven't caught up with his whereabouts—too many other things on my mind—but he could be here. He could be Haye's accomplice."

Randolph turned to her, putting his hands on her face, and she wondered if he needed confirmation that she was still here and not dead like the woman in his memories. "Randolph—"

He kissed her then, cutting off anything else she might have said. Stunned, she let it happen, welcoming the warmth of that fire he started—something different from the oppressive heat of the day—something that wanted to erase any chill inside her, to chase away the hurt and pain and loneliness and replace it with a soothing sensation—maybe he was like tea, though he'd hate that comparison.

"Another minute and I'd be struggling for air," she teased as he let go. "What was that? A confirmation? You know I'm real and alive again? Or were you trying to take a lesson from your cat and mark your territory?"

He shook his head. "You are no one's to claim, despite what Katya thinks."

"How come you did the inappropriate kiss here and not back at the other house, then? I know something's going on in your head, but I don't know what it is. If it's something for the case, you know you should tell me. If it's about the old one, I am here to listen. If it's about... us... It really isn't the time, but we could at least find a comfortable place to leave it until the chaos is over. If you're afraid of losing me—"

"You're the bait, Persephone. That's not going to change. It's just... Knowing what I do about these types of people, about what they're willing to do, about what he would do to you—my hands are tied in a metaphorical sense, and it's hard not to go back to when they were, literally, tied—chained—and I hate this sense of helplessness because he will come after you, and there's nothing I can do to stop it."

"We could both quit the case and run off, get married, and live in the middle of nowhere with a leopard, pretending the rest of the world doesn't matter." She suggested, shrugging. Katya gave a low purr. Persephone shook her head. "Yeah, right, cat. You like going after the bad guys, too."

Katya licked her hand, and Persephone rolled her eyes. Randolph smiled, but she couldn't help noticing that he was still touching her, still afraid to let go. She leaned against him for a moment. "What else are you thinking? Don't you want to know what she's telling them?"

"She's dead," Randolph said, his voice quiet and troubled. He put his arm around Persephone, holding her against him as she tried to wrap her mind around what he'd said. "The girlfriend. She's dead."

"You're sure?"

"She outlived her usefulness. He got rid of her. Not here. Probably somewhere within the state or just across the closest border. Yes, out of state, where they might not have connected her to this. Probably left her clothed—still by a trashcan because that's how he sees all the women he uses—and used a different gun or way of killing her, trying to keep it from connecting to him, but he already got rid of her."

Persephone winced. "Not another one. I mean, I guess I'm glad she didn't actually help him other than the times she lied for him, but... Even if she was an idiot about him, she didn't deserve to die."

"He does," Randolph whispered, closing his eyes for a moment. Persephone knew there was more he wasn't telling her.

"Randolph, spit it out already. What is it?"

"An idiotic idea of how to force his hand. I don't like it, and it would—It is best forgotten."

Persephone wasn't sure if she wanted to push for that one or not. She looked back toward the house. "If she's dead and he dumped her body already, why is Marcie taking so long?"

Chapter Sixteen

"What aren't you showing us? Did he have pictures of me all over the walls in her basement or what?" Reynolds demanded, folding her arms over her chest and studying Marcie. The Italian knew he was caught, and that made him look guilty. "You know you can't hide them from me. If what Randolph says is true, this guy has been building up to going after me, and he'd *have* to stalk me for that. I already know about it, so even if it's hard to see, I will see it."

Marcie sighed. "Look, Reynolds, knowing is one thing. Seeing is another. That's something Randolph knows quite a bit about. Should have seen him when he first got a look at the guy's photo collection."

"I think I vomited," Randolph admitted. "And that was after the man was dead, and I already knew he'd been stalking me."

"Randolph, exactly how fragile do you think I am?" she demanded, moving past him. Katya followed after her.

Marcie grabbed hold of Randolph's arm. "Nothing we could say or do would change her mind about looking, but you know what it can do to her. Hell, I'm a bit worried about what it will do to you."

"I have an idea, but you won't like it."

"We're not talking about what she's seeing right now, are we?"

Marcie asked, shaking his head. "No, I already don't like it. I can tell just by the way you look right now. Whatever it is, drop it and go be there for her. I'll pick up the pieces if I have to, but this idea of yours—forget it."

Randolph just shook his head. The plan was already in the works, whether Marcie liked it or not. His friend would have to accept it because there was no way that he was allowing her to be that bastard's target, not if he could do anything about it. This was a small step, would not make much of a difference, but it was something he was going to do regardless.

He entered the house, hesitating in the doorway. "Reynolds?"

"Back here," she called, and he didn't like what he heard in her voice. He walked toward the back bedroom, and as soon as he crossed the doorway, she had grabbed hold of him. "I know we can't—they're evidence—but tell me we can burn them."

"In the largest bonfire you've ever seen," he agreed, familiar with the reaction. She nodded against his chest. Katya growled, jumping onto the bed and biting the photo album. "Katya, no. We have to have that, unfortunately. I... I know that there is nothing I can say at this point, Persephone. I cannot make this easier. I know a bit of what it's like, but I can't claim to know exactly what you're going through because it's different for you and—"

She put a hand up over his mouth. "Stop. I don't want another one of your rambling speeches at the moment."

"Maybe I need the rambling speech for my own sake," he began, and she looked at him. He fidgeted, uncomfortable. "I have been here before, after all, and you are not the only one in those pictures. He has been following my progress to some degree since my arrival."

Reynolds looked down at the picture near their feet. The two of them outside the precinct, the kiss for the press. She stopped and picked it up, that and the one next to it where they were walking into her mother's house. "That kiss was a very bad idea."

"I disagree."

"You were annoyed at the time."

"Then, yes, but that had more to do with my... desire to be the one to make the first move in any relationship," he said, and she gave him a look. He shrugged. "After the last one I had was a spectacular failure, allowing myself to be... used, to a degree, I would want more than my usual share of control."

"Usual share?"

"It is a partnership, and it must be equal to work."

She nodded. "That mean you're going to tell me what your plan is?"

"I really don't understand. I thought you hated the idea of using me as bait, Randolph. At least, I thought we all agreed that we weren't going there," Persephone said, tempted to smack the woman trying to put makeup on her. "Look, I don't care who sent you over—you cannot make me look less like death warmed over so don't bother trying. If my hair could take dye, I'd just go black with it and dress like a goth to make it easier—"

"And forgo the white witch aspect? I rather like that, actually."

"I don't like being called 'Frosty.'"

"And I told you, repeatedly, that you're not. I admire both sides of you, and I do not think you need to hide any of it," Randolph said with a shrug. He turned to the makeup artist. "Makeup is unnecessary, though. I would prefer she look natural for the press conference—This is important. Leave."

"But—"

The leopard growled, and the woman fled from the room. Persephone laughed. She knew she shouldn't. "Katya, that was mean. Still, thank you. Now make him explain what his plan is already."

The cat turned to Randolph and then looked back at Persephone with that blink Katya did when she was pretending not to understand. Persephone rolled her eyes. "Why won't you just tell me? I really hate doing the press thing."

"I know. I do not wish to subject you to it, but I can see no better way to accomplish this than in front of the press. I am torn between telling you too much and risking your reaction not being what it should be, but that could really go either way at this point. I do think that this will be the best way of making him act before he's ready."

"Before he has a plan where he can escape, you mean."

"Yes."

Persephone took a deep breath. If Randolph's plan was going to work for that, then she was willing to follow it, to a point, at least. She'd see how the rest of this went first. She knew Marciano had his doubts, too, but he did trust his friend enough to let Randolph take the lead for now. "And the dress? I assume that's a message to him, too, but I really don't feel very professional like this. Besides, it's outside, and I'll get burned if this takes very long. With their questions—"

"Someone else will handle that, and the dress is essential to the message, as is the hat. Arguably, the hat will help prevent some of the sunburn, but it's for much more than that."

"Like the fact that you really like seeing me in them," she grumbled, giving him a dirty look. He smiled at her, and she rolled her eyes. "Okay. Will you at least tell me what you and the leopard had to leave to do?"

"No."

"Why not?"

"It will ruin the surprise, and I am counting on that. Trust me, please, and know that this is not just about the case. It does a bit of...

multitasking, I suppose," he mused, running his fingers through the leopard's fur. Persephone frowned at him, not sure what he was up to, but at this point, she'd already asked him and gotten all the details that he was willing to give her.

"Detective Reynolds? We're ready for you now."

She groaned, but Katya licked her hand, and Randolph kissed her forehead. "You'll be fine. Just remember—this will catch the bastard."

"The leopard still gets to bite him," Persephone said, following the aide out to where the press was waiting. She was very uncomfortable with this, but she did more or less trust Randolph. He was good at what he did, and she would give him the benefit of the doubt here. He had insights into these creeps that she never wanted to have. He could keep that job.

"And now, our own Detective Reynolds is here to brief everyone on the latest developments in the case," Mayor Thompson said, moving away from the podium, all smiles. She forced one of her own as she got close.

"Thank you, Mayor Thompson," she began, taking a deep breath. "We have been—We believe we have identified the man responsible for the rapes of eight women. Two of those women were killed, and we believe a third woman—his girlfriend—is also dead at his hand. He is five foot eight, a hundred fifty pounds, with sandy blonde hair, brown eyes and a scar above his right eye. He usually conceals this

232

with a baseball cap and wears a jacket that looks like a letter jacket. No logo. His name is Glenn Haye, and this is his picture."

She gestured behind her to the screen, and the press erupted with questions, just as she had known they would. She held up a hand, trying to find her place in the notes she'd prepared. This was not working, not for her.

Something bumped her leg, and she looked down at the leopard, realizing that—and not her hand—was what stunned the crowd into silence. "Katya, what are you doing? You're not supposed to be out here. And what do you have in your mouth?"

Persephone knelt down and took the small box out of the cat's mouth, shaking it off a bit before opening it. She choked a little, her eyes searching out Randolph in the crowd. Katya walked over to him, and he looked down at her, pretending to chide her. "Sorry, love, that was supposed to be for later."

Like hell it was. She shook her head as she left the podium, crossing to him. "What is this? How did you even manage to get this?"

"Sold the Plymouth."

"You didn't."

He nodded, taking back the box. "I did. And I know it's a bit impractical, but the way those stones matched your eyes was impossible to ignore. I was rehearsing with Katya, she had to have the box because you're kind of stuck with both of us, so she had to be part of the asking, but it wasn't supposed to be... like this."

"Randolph, I honestly have no idea what to say to you right now."

He pulled her close and kissed her. She heard the box hit the ground and felt him slide the ring on her finger. He'd said this wasn't just about the case, but he had to be kidding. They were not getting married.

"Randolph—"

"Sorry. I got carried away. You know I love the way you look in those hats."

She laughed in spite of everything, aware of the fact that they were being photographed and videotaped. Randolph was right about one thing—This *would* set Haye off. He'd be pissed if he saw Persephone giving another man what she wouldn't give him. "I cannot believe you did this."

"It... It is not how I would have preferred to do it. It should have been a private moment with the three of us, and you wouldn't be so upset right now because you'd know... You'd know how much I meant it."

"You're insane."

"Yes, I am. And I have a leopard. But if you say yes, I can show you my ancestral home in England," he said, toying with a strand of her hair. Katya bumped the back of his legs, and he frowned down at her. "I already kissed her, cat. It's her turn to answer, and you need to give her time to—"

Katya pushed him forward, and he almost fell on top of Persephone. She shook her head as she caught him, but then the leopard was pushing at her legs. Persephone looked down at the cat. "I don't think she'll take anything but yes for an answer."

"Oh, don't marry me because you're scared of my leopard."

"I am *not* scared of your leopard," Persephone shot back, and this time she kissed him. She heard Marciano behind her, up at the podium clearing his throat and trying to get the press to focus on him again. It wasn't going to work—that was part of Randolph's plan. He wanted to make Haye angry by taking his spotlight away from him. "I think we should be alone."

"I completely agree, love."

Chapter Seventeen

Randolph was expecting a barrage of outrage the moment they were back inside, but it did not come. He waited, uncomfortable, knowing that he must have pushed things in the wrong direction. He saw this as the best catalyst for Haye's undoing—a man that much in need of power and control, with a vendetta against Reynolds— Haye would make a move if he thought she'd chosen another man. Reynolds' distance, the aloof ice queen myth, had kept most men far from her, and Haye had not seen anyone as competition before, hadn't seen her break free of his hold on her. Her private life was one she kept to herself, but it had allowed Haye to believe he'd kept her imprisoned with his actions back when she was still in high school. Now that was shattered. It should push him over the edge like they needed.

Persephone stopped and toyed with the ring on her finger. "Should I give this back to you now? You need the car more than I need a ring."

Randolph looked down at his feet. "I admit that a large part of that was deliberately staged for the cameras and the press and for the man I know was watching. Not all of it, though. Katya's part was not—other than her interrupting you with the box. She feels strongly about the two of us being together. She has already shown that."

"I still don't know how to react to this. A part of me is angry, another part of me is scared, and the last part..."

"It had to be more than a kiss. Much, much more. He thought he still had a hold on you because you didn't have a serious relationship, at least not one that was public knowledge. He thought he'd ruined you for all men, and that was not the case. Your being single was not about him. It was mostly about your career, I assume, but he twisted that to think he... won, in that respect."

"And now, with that little thing, we've established that I'm not afraid of men and one loves me enough to make ridiculous gestures in public. He can't control me anymore—even if he wasn't controlling me, just thought he was," Persephone agreed, nodding. "Nice. You have a devious and twisted mind, Randolph, but it works."

He forced a smile. "I was thinking about it outside the girlfriend's house, but the pictures confirmed it."

"The ones of us on the floor. The only ones on the floor. Like he was... angry about them."

"Your pictures were in an album. The ones where we were working together were rejected," Randolph said. He wanted to touch her but didn't know if he dared at this point. "I suppose we should check in with the police on the other side of the border and see if they've found his girlfriend yet."

"No, you're taking me out to dinner."

"I am? Since when?"

"Since you proposed to me on live television," Reynolds said, laughing a little. "You can't bait him like that and fail to follow through. If we go back to working on the case, he'll know it was a trap. He needs to see us acting like a real couple."

"We don't have to act."

"How long have I known you? Four days? Five? I've lost track, but it's only been about a week, and I think it's a bit soon to jump from that to marriage, serial killer or no serial killer, cat or no cat."

"Perhaps. Still, if this is a dinner date, then it is a date. We are going as a couple, and not a fake one for his benefit. I *do* want you, Persephone. I have since your reaction to my blundering remark about your resemblance to the white witch."

She gave him a slight smile. "Since you mentioned the leopard."

Katya started to purr. He laughed, going to Persephone's side and kissing her, making it a gentle one. "It's actually somewhat... It is nice to have this be a part of work since the chemistry was becoming harder and harder to ignore."

She gave him an incredulous look. "Did you realize just how much hesitation there is in every time you touch me?"

Randolph swallowed with a bit of difficulty. "It is not you. Not because of what Haye did—It is another part of my past. I told you how he thought I had to be a part of it, how he forced me to touch her. It... It was very difficult for me to touch any woman without it feeling like a violation—my mother forced me out of it, mostly, but with women I don't know as well, I... I still freeze and go back to that moment."

"Randolph, you are such a mess."

"Agreed."

"I suppose we really couldn't have left her at my mother's. This is going to be a bit of an adjustment," Persephone began, running her fingers through Katya's fur as the leopard eyed her food. "You always eat at these sidewalk cafes?"

Randolph nodded. "Whenever possible, yes. Or I get drive-thru and go to a park. It's not the most ideal way to eat or celebrate—"

"It's fine," she broke in before he could apologize. Any relationship would have been an adjustment, and theirs was... new and unexpected and part done for show. She could admit to herself now that part of the reason she'd kissed him in front of the press the first time was that she didn't think they'd ever get to that point. She'd been curious. He was different, had the accent, and he *was* attractive, physically, at least. She didn't kiss every man who crossed her path, no, but she'd managed to find a way to satisfy her curiosity about him. It could have stayed that way, just one question answered, but it was much more than that, as frightening as the concept was.

"Persephone?"

She let out a breath. "Should have remembered you were a shrink. You always going to pick up on my moods that easily?"

"Maybe. You always going to pull me out of wherever I've drifted off to when I get caught up in work or the past?"

"Partners, hmm?"

"Pretty much," he said, reaching for her hand. "Not just partners, of course, but we both have our roles and strengths, counterpointing each other where it's necessary, where we need it to be, giving each other... balance. Support. Not the most romantic way of phrasing it, though."

Persephone rolled her eyes. "Like I'd really want you sitting there telling me I complete you and breaking into song or something ridiculous like that. You're broken. I'm broken. We both know that. Those little pieces are... fragile, but after so long of holding ourselves together, it's nice to let someone else take that role for just a little while, easier to fix the other person... It's... It's amazing how it feels not to be alone, and I find myself a bit angry—not with you, with me—for pushing everyone away for so long. I didn't have to do that. I had Mom, I had Angie, but even with them, I didn't let them in when it mattered. You, nosy shrink that you are, got past all those walls like they were nothing."

He made a face. "I am not nosy. And technically, I'm not a shrink. That's not what I do. It's a common misconception, though."

Persephone smiled at him. "I think I'm full. We should feed Katya, though. She's been very patient."

"Indeed. And then perhaps we'll make out on your mother's porch like teenagers."

"I never did that."

"I was in boarding school as a teenager—an all boys school, I might add—and I had more to lose if I got caught sneaking out after curfew, so I never did, either. I should very much like to find out what that is like with you, Persephone."

"I might—and I stress this as a *might*—let you get to second base, but don't think you'll get any further than that," she warned him as she stood. "Just because you gave me a ring doesn't make you entitled to anything."

"Of course not. I would never assume so much," Randolph said as he paid the check. She knew that he needed to do it as a part of this whole show they were putting on, but she didn't like it. She could pay her own way, and she knew that—despite selling his car—that he couldn't afford it at this point. Once he got his freelance thing going, he'd be fine, but until then, he should conserve his money. He wrapped his arms around her and whispered in her ear. "You can feed Katya if it'll make you feel better about it."

"I still—"

"You're keeping the ring."

"Randolph—"

"It would never match anyone's eyes like it does yours," he insisted, and she sighed, but he held onto her, and she had to admit— this felt good. For years, that moment with Haye had ruined every kind of touch for her, and it wasn't like Randolph's touch was a magical fix for it, but that hesitation he had gave her enough time to decide if she wanted it or not. She could have said no, and that was what mattered. "Love, I hate to ask this, but... You do have your gun, don't you?"

She nodded, trying not to react in away anyone could see. "Yes. You think he's here?"

"I can feel eyes on me, and I know the difference between someone who's casually interested in a strange man with a leopard and someone who hasn't looked away since he spotted me," Randolph answered, a shiver overtaking him that she felt through his hold. "He's here."

"Marcie had someone watching us—"

"This isn't them."

"I didn't say it was. I was just trying to point out that we should signal them somehow."

Randolph stopped, turning her around in his arms. She frowned a little, watching him nod to the leopard. Persephone started to ask him about it, but he kissed her, and as much as she didn't want it to, almost all thought left her head. All she could think about was the way he touched her, the way he tasted—how he was *nothing* like tea at the moment—and she could almost forget that they were standing on the street in the middle of town and there was a rapist and killer watching them. Almost. Not completely.

She tried to pull away, and Randolph held her tighter. Oh. She should have seen it before. They were the distraction. He'd sent Katya after Haye. They had to give the leopard time to track him down. If Haye was focused on them, if he was angry about seeing Persephone with Randolph, then Katya could get close without Haye even seeing her. It was a risk, though, and Persephone was surprised that Randolph had let Katya take it.

"This is like one of those movies," she muttered, and Randolph laughed against her lips before moving on to her neck. She stiffened. "Not there—Randolph, not there."

He nodded, though choosing to work on her ear wasn't much better. "Think you can handle it if I get a little... forward?"

She felt his hand drifting lower. "How far are you planning on taking this?"

"I had actually expected to provoke him a lot sooner," Randolph admitted. She frowned, and then it all seemed to go to hell at once. She heard yelling—maybe even screaming—mixed in with gunshots. First one, and Randolph shoved her down, hard enough to where she figured she'd have bruises on her back where she landed. She tried to track where the shot had come from, pulling away from Randolph and taking out her own gun as she used the nearest car for cover, bullets impacting the metal, forcing her to keep her head down.

"Did you see where that came from?"

"No. Somewhere behind me."

She rolled her eyes. "Someone was thinking with the wrong head there."

He didn't comment as she looked out, still trying to figure out where Haye was. He was no marksman, and she knew if he hadn't been unsettled he would never have tried shooting at her. Besides, he wanted her alive first. Where was Katya? Had the bastard hurt her again?

"Stay there," Marciano called to them. "Should have him cornered in the alley."

"I kind of wanted to shoot him, Marcie."

"Hey, just 'cause you're marrying my best friend doesn't mean you get to use that name," he objected, and she shrugged as she rounded the other side of the car. She didn't care what Marciano thought. She needed to be there for this part. She had to see Haye get arrested, have her moment where she looked that bastard in the eyes and made sure he knew he was never getting out of there. She'd do everything she could to keep him in there to rot. It might not be quite as satisfying as pulling the trigger, but it would be something.

"Didn't realize you were the one watching us," she told Marciano as she joined him. "A team or two, maybe, but you?"

"Other teams would have missed Randolph's signal with the leopard."

"Right. Are we sure Haye is in this alley?"

"Had the other units try to close off the back, but there's no outlet. He's there," Marciano answered, his voice tight. "You'd probably set him off again, just hearing your voice and knowing he missed."

"You want me to talk to him?"

"Nah. Talk to the leopard."

Persephone grinned, following Marciano a bit into the alleyway, moving up to the nearest trashcan, keeping it between them and Haye. "Katya? Where are you, sweetie? It is time to go to Grandma's and get food, remember? Unless you've already eaten, I guess."

Marciano tried not to snicker. The leopard came back to them, limping a little. Persephone moved over to take a look at her. "Did he hurt you again? You did maul him good, right?"

The leopard leaned against her, and she started to look at the cat's injured foot, jerking in surprise when Marciano's Glock went off three times. She rose and looked behind her. He touched her shoulder. "Sorry. I know you wanted to shoot him, but I guess it was my turn."

Persephone walked over to Haye, looking down at him and shaking her head. "I don't... He actually made it back on his feet after that? I mean—It looks like she practically castrated him."

Marciano nodded, studying the mess for a minute. "Would have shot you, too, but I got him first. You okay?"

"Numb, I think," she admitted. "Hasn't sunk in that's really over yet. It will. Once Katya's been checked out, and we connect him to all of this and make sure it's all wrapped up."

"Let Batscher handle that," Marciano said, leading her away from the body, the leopard joining them, still limping. "You have a wedding to plan."

"Very funny."

Marciano smiled at her. Katya moved ahead of them, rubbing her head against Randolph's leg as he leaned against the car Persephone had used for cover earlier. "And I see you managed to get out of doing any of the work again."

Randolph laughed a little. "I did my part."

"Yeah, good plan. It worked."

"This was a plan?" Persephone asked, shaking her head as she joined him against the car. "We need to get someone to look at Katya. She got hurt again."

"I think the hospital will have an easier time with her the second go round."

"The hospital?"

"I told you—I did my part," Randolph repeated, slumping against her. She tried to prop him back up, and Marciano caught his other side. She choked at the sight of the dark stain on his shirt. Blood. The idiot had gotten himself shot protecting her.

Chapter Eighteen

"You know I wouldn't have forgiven you if you'd died. I wouldn't thank you. I'd be angry and curse you for it for the rest of my life. I would never have forgiven you for that."

Randolph reached for her hand, trying to wrap his fingers around it, but they didn't want to cooperate. He sighed as she pulled away, folding her arms over her chest, glaring at him. "I'm not kidding, Randolph. I don't want anyone dying for me, and I didn't need—you didn't have to take a bullet for me, damn it."

"Yes, I did."

She shook her head. "No, because we both know that bastard wanted me alive so he could finish what he started, and that did not mean that you had to—"

"I keep trying to tell you—I couldn't let you become the woman in my head, that voice always asking me for help I couldn't give.. Not you, Persephone. You mean too much to me, and it kills me having a stranger there, but you... I couldn't do it again. Couldn't be that helpless, couldn't sit back and watch and hope we caught him in time. I knew what had to be done—knew how we could provoke him—and I knew what he was likely to do if we did. Yes, I put myself in the way of that bullet, and I would do it again because there was no way I could lose you."

She swallowed hard. "And if I lost you? What about that?"

"You'd take care of my leopard?"

Persephone shook her head, tears escaping her eyes as she tried to control the sobs. "You idiot. I don't understand. For such a smart man, you were so—"

"I had to do it. If I hadn't tried, if I'd left it up to everyone else... That was never an option. It was my hope that Katya would find him before he got off a shot, and we both knew that he was an amateur when it came to firearms—clearly, since the shot that got me was practically a fluke—and I tried to weigh everything I could when I made the choice, but you won't get me to change my mind. That was what I had to do. I... I need you too much to let anything happen to you, and I knew how close I was to shutting down because I could feel that same damn helplessness closing in on me. I swore that was never happening again, and if that meant taking a bullet, it's... It's a small price to pay to know that I did everything I could."

"Randolph," she began, and he caught her hand this time, pulling her close enough to wrap his arm around her on his good side. He kissed her forehead and held onto her for a moment. "You're never ever doing that to me again."

He laughed. "Well, as far as I'm concerned, even with your job, there should *never* be a situation where you're the target of a serial rapist and murderer. It would be my hope that we do not encounter anything like this again."

She looked up at him. "You're not allowed to get yourself killed for me no matter what situation it is. I don't care. It is never going to come to that. It's not a partnership if one of us dies."

"It is, officially, a partnership, then?"

"Are you sure getting yourself shot wasn't part of your plan to make sure I wouldn't say no?"

Randolph snorted. "I figured you'd shove the ring back at me the moment we were alone. I thought you'd be angry that it was even remotely caught up in the case, that I'd hurt you by asking then, and I agree that it is... sudden. I kept trying to tell Katya that I wasn't marrying you just because she claimed you, but—"

"But the leopard always wins."

He shook his head. "If it was only about the leopard, it wouldn't work. There is something between us, though, Persephone, and it is something that can be built upon, something to grow into a lifelong partnership. That is... If you can accept a broke profiler with nothing but a leopard to his name."

"His very pompous name," she said, running a finger across his chest. "Does anyone ever call you Dalton or is it always Randolph?"

"Dalton is generally reserved for my father. Even my mother calls me Randolph."

"You're kidding."

"No. Dalton belongs to the wanker who led her on. Randolph is her prized son. It's how she keeps us separate," Randolph insisted. "I do plan on introducing you to her—she's a very formidable woman, but we'll have to save that for when I'm back on my feet again."

"You want to take me home to your mother?"

"I already asked you to marry me. You'll have to meet my mother eventually. I do believe your mother had long since accepted this... arrangement between us—she did so before we did."

"Probably. She even accepted the leopard."

"So the only thing left to settle is the dress?"

"And getting you out of the hospital."

"No, no, no. Do not bring any more flowers into this already overcrowded and obnoxious room. They are not at all wanted or needed or even viable given their current arrangement, and I will not be subjected to another odorous bouquet of—"

"Randolph," Reynolds said at the same time as the leopard growled at him. He stopped, frowning. His eyes shifted to the person behind the unwanted flowers, and he had to curse himself for his words. He'd only seen her picture in the files, but he knew who she was. Mandy Berkeley. The woman who'd actually spoken to Haye in that parking lot and felt she had to lie about it because people might think she'd encouraged him. Damn it.

She poked her head out a bit from the bouquet. "Is the pain bothering you?"

He winced, wishing one of them had managed to warn him sooner. He hadn't meant to snap at her. He'd thought it was another one of Marcie's vases, sent just to annoy him while he was stuck in this bed. Randolph tried to sit up, letting out a breath in a hiss. "I fear it is more my dislike of hospitals. I am a terrible patient. I... I hope my mood was not too... distressing for you. I'm sure it wasn't easy to walk in to my room, and I apologize for my rudeness."

Mandy forced a smile. "I didn't really know what to expect when I saw you. We never met before."

He grimaced. "I was—"

"Busy?"

He laughed. "Perhaps a few years ago that might have been my reason, but no. I must call it cowardice. I am afraid I thought seeing any of you would trigger my own PTSD. That, and I would have spared you my presence, knowing how difficult that would be for you after what I have seen and experienced."

She frowned. "What, some creep do that to you?"

"No, mercifully, he did not. He... made me watch. Tried to get me to be a part of it."

She almost dropped the vase. Reynolds took it from her, setting it next to the bed. Katya, at least, had the good sense to intervene and circled around to offer her services as a therapy cat. The girl put her hand in the leopard's fur, and the cat began a soothing sort of purr. "So... Why do this? Why work our case?"

He pointed to the cat. "The leopard."

"Very funny."

It wasn't completely inaccurate, but he shrugged. He had taken the case mostly because of his near desperate circumstances—ones brought on by the leopard—but he had other reasons for staying and seeing it through to the end despite threatening to quit as many times as he had. "To help stop him. I can't undo what he did to you, but I do get some satisfaction in knowing that I could prevent him from doing more."

She bit her lip. "I wish they could have called you in sooner."

He didn't want to get into the politics and policies that went into asking for his kind of help. He shook his head. "I don't know that I could have done anything without the clear pattern that was evident when I arrived. I'm... You needn't have brought the flowers. I didn't earn them. Unless, of course, they are for the leopard, in which case she may well eat them in her enthusiasm."

Mandy laughed, then frowned. He knew that sort of reaction, the surprise to find himself laughing after what he'd seen or done. The first few times—first few smiles, too—were always a bit awkward. "You were both a part of stopping him, in making sure that he... Well, you know... I can't help being glad that he's gone. I think the others must be, too. Arresting him would have been something, but it's better that he's dead."

Randolph shifted in the bed, trying to ease the ache in his side with a better position. "I definitely had nothing to do with that."

"You got shot before then."

He nodded. "My one real contribution to the affair."

Reynolds rolled her eyes. "Modesty doesn't become you, Randolph. You know you were a huge part in figuring this thing out and making sure he didn't get away with it."

"I am no hero, Persephone."

Mandy shook her head. "It's not so much about that. I don't want a hero. It's just—I was able to leave the house today. That... It matters. More than you know."

Randolph bit back his response to that. No, he'd never been violated, but he knew a lot more than she thought. He'd been a real mess after that shovel. Even without that, he was a profiler. He knew. "I'm glad you were able to get out of the house. I hope that things continue to improve for you."

"Thanks. You... Uh, can give the flowers to the leopard if you really hate them."

"I think I'll keep them. No sense in giving the leopard a bigger head than she's already got."

"Not a bad place for a barbecue," Marciano commented, leaning back in the lawn chair with a beer, giving Randolph a broad grin. Lillian gave him a smile before turning back to the grill, flipping the burgers. Randolph didn't comment—His eyes were closed, once again he was half-asleep thanks to the painkillers the doctors had prescribed him when they let him out of the hospital.

Persephone looked up at the sun. "I hate barbecues."

"Only because you're terrified of getting burned, love," Randolph said, making a blind reach for her hand. She gave it to him rather than let him keep flailing. Katya lifted her head from the ground and moved it into his lap again. "I'm fine, Katya. Don't even feel the pain because of the drugs—Still no hugs, though. We've discussed this. I can't take your weight at the moment."

The leopard licked his other hand, and he sighed.

"When are you leaving, Marcie?"

Marciano shook his head again at Persephone's use of the

nickname, but she just shrugged. "All the last bits of the case are being typed up and filed—we nailed him as much as we ever would have been able to, and we found his girlfriend, so we're pretty sure all the loose ends have been wrapped up, finally. We all know it isn't over for the live victims, but they're on the road to recovery now, and they can sleep a bit easier knowing he can't ever hurt them again. That's the best we can do. So, tomorrow I head back to my loving wife and regular job, but I'll be back as soon as Randolph's really on his feet again, with the wife, because we're not missing the wedding."

Randolph groaned, and Persephone laughed. "You asked. This is kind of your fault."

"I blame the leopard."

"Oh, please. You love each other," Lillian scoffed as she handed Marciano a plate. He smiled at her in thanks, and she went back to the grill. "No arguing. You didn't get shot for my daughter out of a sense of duty, and if she didn't love you back, that ring would never have made it on her finger."

"Can't win with mothers or leopards."

"Should be interesting when your mother joins this mess," Marciano observed, taking a bite out of his burger.

"Don't scare them with horror stories of my mother now," Randolph warned. "They'll think she's the harbinger of doom the way you go on about her. You'll make poor Persephone want to elope and

Lillian will regret accepting me and the leopard, thinking she'll have to deal with the impossible for the rest of her life."

"Hey, you're the one bad mouthing your mother now. I didn't say a word."

Randolph turned and glared at him. "You hate my mother, and you know it."

"She's scary."

"Only to a man whose mother never had the need to leave the house and seek employment. The fact that my mother is an extremely successful business woman terrifies you."

"I married a very liberated woman, I'll remind you."

"Partially because her cooking rivals your mother's."

"Shut up, *Dalton.*"

"Katya, go bite him."

"Boys!" Lillian intervened, though she was fighting laughter like everyone else. Persephone smiled as she leaned against Randolph's shoulder. She enjoyed watching him interact with his friend. It was good, practically priceless. "Behave."

"Yes, Mrs. Reynolds," Randolph said, even as Marciano mouthed, "Never."

Lillian sighed. She took a deep breath. "What about the job situation? Is the department here hiring you full time as a consultant?"

Persephone snorted. "Like they'd ever approve that in the budget.

The mayor already thanked him personally for his help with the case, the invaluable public service, and then tried to shortchange him on the fees. It should be interesting dealing with the hospital bills after this."

"If worst comes to absolute worst, I will ask my mother for a short term loan. I am not worried. Beyond her, of course, there is my father, but I am confident that my current financial difficulties are temporary. I do have skills I can use, and actually, I did get a call from someone I used to work with asking me to take a look at something, and I will when I'm not on drugs that make thinking nearly impossible."

"You didn't ask her for money before."

"I don't ask anyone for money. I'm stubborn that way. And I know that I can make a living without assistance," Randolph insisted. He put a hand to his head. "It'll be fine. Like I said, I have resources I can turn to if I need to, but I'd much rather live by my skills and my wits than ask my parents for anything. Especially after my mother worked as hard as she did to make sure that everything other than my tuition was covered. No, I can redeem my finances, and I will. I'll even do it before the wedding if necessary."

"I don't care if you have money or not," Persephone told him. "I believe you'll do just fine as a freelance consultant."

"You'd make a good team—the two of you and the leopard," Marciano added. They looked at him. "Think about it. You could make it a business, too. I have a hard time seeing Reynolds being happy about you leaving her behind, and the leopard won't know what to do if you separate. Just turn it into a package deal because you already are one."

"Is that so?" Randolph asked Persephone.

She nodded. "Yeah, I think we kind of are."

"You overslept, love."

Persephone frowned as she opened her eyes, looking up at Randolph as she did. He shouldn't be on his feet. Though, for her, the strange thing was seeing the sunlight creeping in through the window behind him. "I *never* oversleep. I barely even sleep. You know that."

Randolph shrugged, kneeling down to brush back a part of her hair. "Perhaps a part of what kept you from sleeping was also knowing that Haye was out there, free. He's not free now. He's dead."

"I know he's dead. I went back to the morgue twice, just to be sure," she said, sitting up. "I can't believe I fell asleep in here again. I was more than ready to leave this bedroom behind."

He sat down next to her. "We did talk late into the night despite my medication. And Katya was pretty insistent that you not leave. She is still quite torn by this separation idea. She does not care for it at all."

"It's not going to last too much longer," Persephone reminded him—and the leopard, who put her head in his lap. Persephone started to pet her, laughing a bit as he reached out to the cat at the same time. "Not if we do go ahead with this consulting business."

"I thought you liked the idea."

"I actually do," she said. Even with BB's apology and improved attitude, she preferred working with Randolph, and she knew he needed someone to look out for him on the job as well. He would get lost in his thoughts or memories if someone wasn't there to pull him back. Besides, she was a good investigator in her own right. "I know we have to wait a bit before that, need to build your reputation and stabilize a few things financially before we really make it a business. Mom keeps saying we could move in here and cut the expense of my apartment."

"I am aware of that."

Persephone frowned at his tone. "You don't like my mother?"

"It is not that."

"Your mother?"

"She might not understand why we would live with your mother and not her," he said, sounding reluctant as he toyed with Persephone's hair again, getting lost in thought as usual. She caught his hand and drew him back to the present.

"How does your mom do with the leopard?"

Randolph shuddered. "Too well. There is a reason I didn't move back in with her after I lost the apartment. I need some illusion of my own life. With her and the cat, there would have been no room for me."

Persephone nodded. She could understand that. She had her reasons for not living with her mother as well. She knew that Lillian wanted them both here, but Persephone didn't intend to move back in, even if they needed to work out the financial end of their partnership—she wanted space, *needed* it. "Mom is making coffee. You want help getting downstairs?"

"No, I'm fine. If need be, there's Katya. I'll see you downstairs after you shower," he said, kissing her cheek and rising, still a bit stiff. Persephone sighed. She hated seeing him struggle, and she wished that he had not thought he had to risk himself to save her. It was a good thing that Haye *was* dead. She did kind of feel like vandalizing his grave, though.

She shook off that thought as she went into the shower, making it a quick one. She was running a bit late, but she didn't care too much about that—with Haye dead, things had settled back into the usual routine around the precinct—and she figured that the consulting idea was also appealing because ever since she got back it was almost *too* easy at work. She wasn't sure she could settle into that again.

She finished in the shower, drying off and dressing with enjoyment for a change. She used another one of her lighter long sleeved shirts, the thin cotton ones that Randolph had talked her into, thinking that she would like to throw out the dress code—another reason to like the idea of going into consulting work with her future husband.

She walked downstairs, running her fingers through her hair. Something black shot past her, forcing her to grab the rail so that she didn't fall. She frowned. "Katya? What's with you?"

"She's here."

"She?"

Randolph went to the door and opened it so that the cat wouldn't shred it in her attempt to get it open. He smiled at the woman standing there. "Hello, Mother."

"Randolph," the woman said, shaking her head as she pulled him down for a kiss on each cheek before turning to Katya and spouting a bunch of incoherent babble at the leopard that made her purr. "I see someone missed me."

"Only because you spoil her rotten, Mother."

The woman made a tsking noise with her tongue, moving into the house. She smiled as she looked around, nodding in what Persephone took as approval. She wouldn't have picked her for Randolph's mother, though. He must have been a near replica of his father because there was almost no sign of relation in them. The woman was shorter, with much lighter hair and brown eyes. The eyes were not shaped the same, the nose was wrong, and Persephone couldn't see any resemblance.

"Oh, you must be Persephone," the woman said, clapping her hands together before she reached the stairs, taking hold of her and hugging her close. "You are an absolute beauty. Randolph has not done you justice—and yet I thought he had to have been exaggerating."

"Excuse me? I did *not* exaggerate—"

"You're very lovely," the other woman went on, ignoring her son. "I'm sure you've heard a few horror stories about me by now, but I assure you—they're all true."

Persephone found herself laughing. "Well, Marcie seems intimidated."

"He would be."

"Mother, please stop crowding her. You don't need to fuss."

"Am I fussing?"

Persephone shrugged, feeling a bit helpless. "I don't know. I have to go to work, actually. I'm late, so... Please excuse me, Mrs. Ran— No, wait, your name wouldn't be Randolph."

"Just call me Margaret. Don't worry about the last name. We'll have to discuss the wedding when you get home."

Persephone forced a smile and nodded, but she had no intention of doing that. She moved toward the door. Randolph caught her arm and leaned down to whisper in her ear. "If you want to elope, now is definitely the time."

She laughed. "It can't be that bad."

"Did I hear the door?" Lillian asked, coming in from the kitchen. She saw Margaret and stopped. "Oh, hello. I'm Lillian Reynolds. Persephone's mother. And you are... Randolph's mother, I assume?"

"Margaret," the other woman agreed, smiling as she scratched the leopard's ears. "It's good to meet you. You have a lovely home here."

"Thank you," Lillian said with a smile. "It's not much, but I always thought it was kind of cozy."

"Cozy is wonderful. Is that coffee I smell? I could use one after the trip. And I must say, your daughter is an absolutely stunning young lady. I can just picture her in her wedding dress..."

"I know! It'll be so perfect."

"And this would be when we run," Randolph whispered, and Persephone nodded, reaching behind her for the door handle.

"I object to the snowflakes."

Persephone folded her arms over her chest, glaring at him. "What are you doing here, Randolph? You're still not supposed to be walking around, and sneaking into my dress fitting is rather low, don't you think?"

Randolph pointed to the leopard. Katya jumped up onto the counter and started purring. Persephone shook her head. "You can't go blaming everything on the leopard, you know. I thought you were going over the file you were sent and *resting*. Because, in case you've forgotten, you got shot. Shot. That means you don't wander around aimlessly and crash fittings."

"And we don't argue with the leopard. The leopard always wins. Katya took off, I followed, and here we are," Randolph told her, leaning against the wall. "I repeat my objection to the snowflakes. The rest of the dress I love, but snowflakes? You're not the ice queen. Not frosty. Not frigid."

She gave him a look. "You don't know that. A few kisses does not make you an expert. And you can't play the shrink card, either."

"The profiler card," he corrected, moving toward her, putting his hands on arms, keeping his touch gentle. He didn't want to upset her further. "If this makes you uncomfortable, don't do it. Not for my sake or even the leopard's."

Persephone reached up to touch his face. "I would not have agreed to this if I didn't want it. The dress is... symbolic, I suppose, and I'll leave it up to you to figure that one out, Mr. Profiler."

"The death of the myth," he began, studying her. "While someone who does not know you might still make some erroneous conclusions, you see this as an end to that era of stupidity. No more ice queen comments."

"You're the one that says I'm not frosty."

"You're not. And I doubt you're frigid, either. I look forward to proving that—several times over in the course of the rest of our lives," Randolph told her, kissing her. She looked absolutely stunning, and he should *not* have come because she *was* that tempting. He pulled back and shook his head. "I think it fits well enough. Let's go now."

Persephone laughed, leaning her head against his chest for a moment. "We already have it all set, and it's not that far away. Everyone's going to be there. I think you can be patient for a few more days, even with your mother ready to take over everything, and besides, I would prefer it if you weren't injured when you go to take this dress off."

Randolph nodded. "I—That would make sense, yes. Sorry. I told you before you were addicting, but I don't think I actually said how much I love you."

"True, you didn't. We were avoiding those words because of the... speed of this thing. It's supposedly too soon to say it and mean it, but I'd like to believe you do. You did get shot for me, after all," she said, playing with the button on his shirt again.

"I did, but that's not why you're marrying me. More like you're doing that in spite of what I did."

She laughed again. "What were you working on last night that you tried to hide from me?"

"A cold case."

She pulled back and looked at him. "Randolph, did you... Did you profile my father's killer?"

"Not completely. I've got a few theories."

"More crazy ones?"

"Things you can look into, at least."

"What, it's not enough that you somehow managed to disrupt the four hour sleep cycle I had for so long and got shot for me, you have to help me solve that, too?"

"You matter to me. What matters to you matters to me."

"Oh, hell, I think I *do* love you," she said, and he smiled at her just before the leopard bumped her legs and knocked her into him. "I think that's your cue, too."

"I don't need to be prompted to kiss you," he assured her as he did just that.

Bonus Story: When Randolph Met Katya

"You are so overqualified for this, you do realize that."

Randolph smiled as he looked up from his papers. Of course Marcie would say that. He always did. A consistent and faithful companion, Marciano believed that only serial killers and the worst crimes deserved the attention of his friend and profiler. No case was good enough for the other man, nothing worth wasting Randolph's time on unless Marcie picked it out himself. A single murder for the local police force was not the sort of thing that his friend would consider a good use of Randolph's so-called talents, but he liked the simple and straight-forward work something like this offered him.

"This isn't you hiding away because of that case, is it? You haven't worked on anything worthy of your skills in almost six months."

Randolph grunted, setting down his pen. He did not need this. Not now. His head was already threatening to give him one of those ever so pleasant migraines again, and he was not done with this. He had a feeling about it, and he was set to confirm it as soon as he got through these other files, but he hadn't finished making his notes yet.

Marcie sat down on the edge of the desk. "I am not asking you to do the shrink thing on me. I don't want all the sordid details. I just worry about you, *amico.* I can't help it. You haven't been the same since you took that shovel to the head."

"I'm fine. I move a bit slower these days trying not to set off a migraine, but I'm good. I'm working, I'm not hiding in bed or locked inside my apartment. I'm not a shaking, incoherent mess, and I think it is past time we dropped this matter," Randolph said, rising from his desk. The bottle of pills was in his coat pocket, and he needed one now, or he'd lose the rest of the day. He was too close to let that happen. He had to finish this.

"Your accent changed. You're pissed off again."

"Oh, what a fine investigator you are, Marcie."

"Stop that."

"I offer you this truce: I won't call you Marcie if you agree not to bring up that case or the migraines again. I told you I'm fine."

"You're lying, but I'll let it go for now." Marciano let out a breath, shaking his head. Randolph knew this was not over; they'd be discussing this issue for the rest of their lives. Every time he got one of his headaches, he figured his life would end up being rather short, but that was not something he felt like talking about—nor were the nightmares, the flashbacks, or anything to do with his unfortunate but undeniable post-traumatic stress disorder.

"Good," Randolph said, taking the bottle from his coat and

walking back to his desk. "Come over here. I want to see if you see what I do when I was looking at this thing."

"You know I won't. This is revenge, isn't it? Asking me to see what you see? Your mind is... It is a place no one wants to be, and I say that as a friend. Your best friend."

Randolph glared at him for a moment. He turned the cap and pushed it off the bottle, opening it and dumping a pill into his hand. "Look at the pattern. Am I wrong about it?"

Marciano picked up the files, skimming them over, his brow furrowing as he did. "I was wrong, Randolph. This is a case that needed you. I don't know that anyone else would have caught it, but you're always following those crazy thoughts of yours... and it looks like this time you found us a serial killer."

"I didn't find *him.* I have no idea who he is. I'm not psychic. I didn't have a vision, just a sense that the killing was too... perfected to have been this guy's first. I started looking for similar murders, and I found some—they're scattered all over the country, though. This guy travels. A lot."

"Salesman? Business type? What are you thinking?"

"Well... That's what's been bothering me." Randolph reached for his water and swallowed down the pill. "Who travels with a whip, anyway?"

"We're going in here to *talk* to this guy. I mean, we have enough probable cause to get a warrant to search his little tent, but we are only here to talk. Don't get happy—and Randolph, don't wander off."

Randolph glared at Marciano. He was not a child, and it was not wandering that had resulted in his current difficulties. He had been back where he was supposed to be, on the outside, ostensibly protected by the many agents around him, and he had just passed by one when he took a shovel to the back of his head. He didn't need to be treated like he was always in trouble. He was a better shot than Marciano, and he had gone through the same training at Quantico. He was a specialist, not a baby.

"Marcie, this was my idea, my find, and it should be my arrest. If you want to chit-chat under the big top, that is your problem, not mine. I have long since believed that you belonged in a sort of circus, but this is not the time to indulge that whim of yours."

His friend shook his head. He turned to the other agents that had accompanied them. "Ignore him. He's got another migraine. Gather everyone in the main tent, I want them here while we complete the search. We're looking for a dangerous killer. We believe this person has killed at least six people. I want you alert and focused. Be careful. You don't know what you'll find, and I'm not just talking about the house of horrors over there."

Randolph let Marciano drone on with his instructions, leaving the group there. He wanted—perhaps he should say he *needed*—to see this for himself. He had his doubts about their choice—yes, this particular traveling fair had been in the same city or near each of the kills, and the type of weapon favored by the killer was the same as ones used by a group of performers that toured with it. Still, they had no real proof that it had anything to do with this fair or these people. He did not want to stereotype them. Other people used whips—horse trainers, people with certain fetishes, and even a very famous archeologist.

That last one was fictional. He couldn't help bringing up one of the most infamous whip users, though. Anyone would have.

He passed by two horse trailers and a half-dozen scattered other trailers, ones for vending anything from hot dogs to cotton candy, his nose turning up at the smell. He hoped that was the animal waste and not the food, but he would not assume anything. He was here to observe and see if he had been even half-correct in the profile that he had assembled.

He stopped. What was that? That noise... Something unholy, unnatural lived in its wail, and he went for his gun. Taking it out, he moved around the other side of the trailer. He stopped, staring, his stomach heaving worse than it did with one of his migraines.

"Useless animal. Trained? What a laugh. That old man lied.

You're not worth what I paid for you. Thought I was getting a real good deal, but look at you. *Look.*"

The whip snapped, cutting a deep gouge into the cat's side, and Randolph flinched, about to turn away. He couldn't. He already knew that. He shuddered, shaking off the memories. He couldn't allow himself to go into a flashback now. Not that he could prevent them, but he had to try.

"What the bloody hell do you think you're doing?"

Nice, Randolph. What was it you were just saying about not being a child and having training to deal with these things? He supposed it had disappeared the minute his eyes saw that pitiful creature under the man's whip. That poor thing must have been the one to make that noise, and she looked at him with such pain in her eyes. He saw a woman there instead, and he *knew.* Marcie might think that Randolph was confusing past and present, but he was convinced—that man with the whip had killed those women.

The panther was all the proof they needed.

The whip cracked, and Randolph cried out as it stung his skin. He looked at the other man. "Are you insane? I may not have said I was FBI, but I am holding a loaded gun. You have got to be one of the dumbest and cruelest criminals I have ever had the misfortune to come across. Drop the whip, now, or I will have to shoot you."

The man's lips twisted into a sick facsimile of a smile, and he flicked his hand back like he was going to strike again. The cat lifted her head, and he sent the whip right back at her.

Randolph aimed the gun at the man. He'd already given warning enough, and he would rather this butcher be stopped this second, but he was a representative of the law. He had to uphold that authority, not let himself be pushed over the edge by emotion. "I said drop it. This is your last warning. I will shoot you."

"For what? You on some committee with the ASPCA or something?"

"No. You're under arrest for murder. Or did you think no one would connect you to the six women you whipped and tortured to death? What was it, exactly? A form of—No, no, you need to feel dominant, don't you? You need to feel bigger and stronger, but all you are is a pathetic bully. No one is impressed by your 'show.' You're nothing, and when you die after many, many long years rotting in prison, no one will remember you."

"You got nothing on me."

"You're holding the evidence in your hand, moron."

The trainer looked down at his whip. He snarled, and Randolph saw him raise the whip. The man was not going to stop. He might figure he could knock the gun out of Randolph's hand, or he might just be setting himself up for a suicide by cop. Either way, Randolph didn't have a choice. Warnings issued and ignored, he had to fire—and he wasn't sure if it mattered if the man stood trial or not.

He squeezed off a shot, then a second, watching the man stumble back, falling to the ground. Good. He was down. Randolph kept the gun on him, stepping forward until he reached the other man. The trainer's chest was still moving up and down, so maybe he would stand trial. Randolph kicked the whip out of the other man's hand, not wanting to pick it up without gloves.

He would wait. The others would have heard the shots, and they would be here soon enough.

Something bumped his leg, and he looked down. "Oh, love, you shouldn't be on your feet. You need to rest and gain your strength. You're rather done in, I should think."

The cat leaned against him, weak and yet determined to have his attention, and he knelt down to pet the poor thing's head. "Easy now. Rest. Just stay still."

She growled, and he shook his head. Silly kitty. She would injure herself further. "I think you should—"

The whip went over his head and tightened against his neck before he realized that he'd heard something behind him. His hands went up to free himself, losing his gun to tug on the cord. He should have shot the bastard a third time, but the shots had not missed, and the man was down. He should have stayed that way.

The cat leapt at the trainer, taking a rather large bite out of his leg.

The whip came loose, and Randolph yanked it off, falling forward as he caught his breath. He looked back in time to see another shot knock the trainer to the ground.

"Am I always going to have to save you from yourself? Why the hell did you think I told you not to wander off, Randolph?"

He rubbed his neck. "The cat saved me, not you. And it wasn't like I could have waited—he might have killed her before I got here. Come here, love. That's it. Just lie down and rest now. You're safe. He won't hurt anyone ever again."

"No, he won't," Marciano said. "I'll call an ambulance."

The cat looked at him, a terrible and pitiful look, and he sighed. He ran his fingers through the cat's fur and turned to Marciano. "We need a vet, too. Someone has to see to the real hero."

Marcie grunted. "You be careful now, *amico.* I don't think your apartment takes pets."

"Don't be ridiculous. This sort of animal belongs in the wild. As soon as she's healed, she'll go back to her natural habitat."

"Sure she will. How do you even know it's a she?"

"Oh, well, I... Educated guess?"

"Sir? Can we get a look at your neck?"

Randolph looked at the EMT and nodded. He did not want it, but they wouldn't let him leave without it, not with Marcie around. His friend would be obsessing over how close this came to the last time, about how it would affect the PTSD, and he would be as insufferable and paranoid as he had been since the shovel incident. Randolph was not looking forward to being smothered under the agent's well-meaning but irritating protection again.

The paramedic came closer, setting down his pack. The cat lifted her head and growled. Randolph frowned at her. He gave her head another pat, but when the EMT opened his bag, she rose and put herself in between the man and Randolph, baring her teeth.

The other man froze. "Uh, nice kitty..."

She snarled. Randolph shook his head. "Stop that. He's only trying to help, and while I personally do not believe I need medical attention, you have to let him examine me. Come on, love, let the man do his job."

The cat regarded the paramedic, suspicion in her eyes, and then she turned back to Randolph. He nodded, holding out his hand to her. She limped over to it and rubbed her head against his palm. "There. That's better. You sit here and rest, and we'll get you your own doctor very soon. Marcie, I thought you called the vet. Where is he?"

"They don't have a bunch of them ready to go in fancy machines like they do for us humans, and the first three I spoke to told me they couldn't help a panther. When the fourth one told me I was looking at a leopard, not a panther, I figured even if she wasn't an expert, she was the one. Turns out she studied zoology, too, and she said I should ask one of them—"

"No. Not a zoo. They'll want to keep her in captivity, and she has suffered enough," Randolph said, scratching the cat's ears. "A leopard? Is she sure?"

"Most of them are, I guess. Panther's a common misconception because of the color. Or so I'm told." Marciano studied the cat for a moment. "I don't know, Randolph. A zoo might be a better place for her. They do have people trained to take care of the animals, and more and more of them are going toward these bigger, more natural habitats—"

"You want to subject a cat who has been nearly whipped to death to more human interaction? I think that would be a bad idea."

Marciano nodded. "I get that, but it's not like you can put her back in the wild, either. It's possible she's too domesticated for that."

The EMT forced Randolph's head up, examining his neck. "Did you lose consciousness at all?"

"No. The welt is the worst of it, and I expect it shall fade soon enough. I do not need overnight monitoring."

Marciano grunted. Randolph ignored him. He did not want to hear it. He had only been under that whip for a minute, and while he didn't doubt that if he hadn't shot the trainer before the man made that attempt he'd be dead, he had. The man was too injured to pull off a quick strangulation, and the cat had intervened. Randolph was alive. He was fine.

"He should be monitored. Don't send him home with a clean bill of health."

"I don't have a migraine right now. I am just a bit sore. Also a bit chagrined. I should not have turned my back on him, but I had incapacitated him with two shots and disarmed him. How was I supposed to know he was going to act out a horror film ending on me?"

The cat bumped his arm. "Oh, I see. You would have told me that. Is that why you wouldn't rest? Well, you need to communicate better. I had no idea."

"Have you listened to yourself in the past few minutes, Randolph? You are talking to that leopard like... a person. Like she understands."

"She might."

"I think we should have you monitored overnight."

"Doctor, how is your patient?"

"She's been very restless. I haven't been able to do much to keep her calm, at least not by natural means. I'm reluctant to over-medicate her. I think keeping her pain managed is the best option, but I don't think she'll be willing to let us keep her here much longer."

Randolph could not blame the leopard for that. He had not wanted to enter the place himself. He understood that most vets did not have the necessary experience to deal with a large cat like her. They had taken her to the local zoo, and he cringed walking into their treatment facility. He was used to human hospitals, clean run facilities with extreme organization. He did not know what to think of this. Not because he thought there was any neglect going on—he would never have let the cat stay here if he did—but because it was not what he expected.

"You want to see Kitty?"

He grimaced. "Who named her that? You cannot call a magnificent creature like that something as mundane and ordinary as 'Kitty.' That belongs to a house cat, maybe, but a leopard?"

The vet laughed. "Well, that's what they told us her name was, Mr. Randolph. The carnival did not have a great deal of information regarding her, since she was apparently a new acquisition that the so-called lion tamer had purchased only a short while ago from an older act that had gone out of business and whose owner had very poor health. We tried contacting him, but he had passed on, and so we unfortunately have little to go on respecting her health and prior treatment, but I would say she was probably well cared for before this trainer."

"That is a relief."

"Here she is now," the vet said, pushing open the door. She smiled at the leopard. "She likes to mangle her pillows like that. We're not sure why."

"She likes them fluffy, don't you, Katya?"

"Katya?"

"A term of endearment for one named Kitty, or so I understand from the Tolstoy translation I read." He caught the woman's look and shook his head. *"Anna Karenina,* the better part of the story. A second plot line overlooked by many, a quiet little journey of self-discovery and romance between Levin and Kitty. He called her 'Katya.'"

"Oh."

The leopard bumped against his leg, and he frowned down at her. "You should be resting, you know. How are you ever going to get well enough to go back to the wild if you don't?"

The cat blinked. She nudged his hand with her head, purring. The vet frowned, adjusting her ponytail as she watched them. "I think she'd rather be with you, Mr. Randolph."

"Ah, well, I am sure my girlfriend would object to that—and if not her, certainly my landlady." He knelt down to the cat's level. "You should be free to roam about, and you'd never be happy in the city. I think wide spaces suit someone of your importance and stature, don't you?"

The leopard put her paws on his legs and knocked him over. He sat up with a frown, and then the cat crawled on top of him. She must have been at least two hundred pounds of dead weight, and he was not going anywhere. "Um, Katya..."

The cat closed her eyes, still purring, but he swore the damn thing had gone to sleep on him. Great. Now he was the bloody pillow.

"That is the most she has stayed in one spot since she came here—other than when she was sedated. You seem to do a good job of calming her—perhaps your accent reminds her of the man she used to live with or something. Would you mind coming by again? It might help her recover faster if we can keep her still."

"Can we do this with me on a couch or something? Not on the floor? I don't fancy sitting on this hard surface for any length of time."

"Of course. We'll figure something out."

"I thought you said you took the cat to the nature preserve."

Randolph nodded, too fatigued to argue with his friend. Last month, they'd tried releasing Katya back into the wild, but she wouldn't eat. She wandered off the land and into human settlements, and the zoologists had tried working with her to get her hunting her meals again, but they said it was possible she'd never do that. She was *too* domesticated. They weren't certain she could take care of herself out there, and after the other leopards started fighting with her, they had taken her back to the zoo, afraid she was going to get herself killed. She lacked the survival skills she needed for the wild.

He didn't believe that. He did not think Katya wanted to be there, and everyone knew she did not want to be in that zoo. So he had made other inquiries, found a nature preserve dedicated to cats and other animals just like her, and he arranged to take her there.

"Why is the cat sitting at your feet if you took her to a preserve? Did you chicken out? I know you like her, *amico,* but you cannot keep her."

"I'm not trying to keep her. Honest. I left her there, but when I got home, she was waiting by the front door."

"She ran back here faster than you drove?"

"Granted, she is no cheetah, but she can run at almost fifty miles an hour if she so desires. With me stopping for lunch and slowing down for those smaller towns along the way, it was apparently possible. I dare you to dispute the proof sitting right next to you."

Marciano frowned. "I see. Well, you know, they tell epic tales of dogs returning home to their masters or those dogsled races to get the medicine and save the children, but... a leopard?"

"I think I have been... claimed, Marcie. She wants to be with me, and she will not accept the alternative. When returned to her natural habitat, she acted as though... depressed. She would not hunt, she would barely eat, and she found her way into human settlements—possibly looking for me. After that failure and her refusal to stay in that wilderness preserve..."

The other man eyed the leopard. "You think she'll just keep coming back?"

"Yes."

"You could try to get special license to keep her in the city, but it won't be easy. Then on top of that is the cost of the thing—how much *does* she eat? You won't be able to afford an apartment. Oh, and there's the job thing to consider."

"That shouldn't be an issue. I don't go into the field that much, and I can do plenty from my desk. Or from home. I hope, at any rate. If she follows me everywhere—and she has, on occasion—I may be in a great deal of trouble."

Marciano turned to the cat. "You know you can't go making his life miserable. Only I'm supposed to do that."

"Very funny."

His friend shrugged. "You have to start talking boundaries if you're going to keep her."

"I can't keep her. We both know that. She's a wild animal. She's not meant to be kept." The leopard growled. Randolph shook his head. "You know that, Katya. You know you don't belong with people. Yes, a great deal of us like you and care about you, but you are not supposed to be in the middle of a city. It is not the right fit for you— and I shudder to think what some idiot might do to you if he gets scared. You should be out where you can be free."

Katya nudged his hand, and then tried to climb into his lap. "No, you are not just a big kitty. Stop that. You—not the face. Disgusting."

Marciano laughed. "I think she's trying to tell you she likes you. Either that, or she's planning on eating you in your sleep."

"You're not helping."

"Face it, Randolph. You've got a leopard. For better or worse, that cat is yours."

Randolph managed to push the cat off his lap and back to the ground. He sighed as he looked at her. "I don't think she's mine so much as... In her mind, I belong to her. That's what it is. She's claimed me. I'm hers. There's no use fighting it."

The leopard purred.

www.ingramcontent.com/pod-product-compliance
Lightning Source LLC
Chambersburg PA
CBHW070811180626
46818CB00001B/209